W9-BLU-085

He was just as bad as she'd expected him to be

"Your father has made quite a name for himself in schooling difficult horses," Eliot said as he looked around him with a proprietorial air.

"Yes," Natalie agreed, "he's fantastic with horses."

"What a pity one can't apply the same techniques to difficult women." Eliot opened the door with a mocking gesture. He was smiling that falsely gleaming smile of his.

Not for long, Natalie thought. "Tell me, Mr. Lang," she said, her voice poisonously sweet, "are those teeth your own?"

"Indeed they are," he said, smiling. "Would you like me to prove it by biting you?"

"No, I wouldn't," she answered, stepping away from him.

"What a pity," he said, "because it's about time someone made a mark on you, sweetheart."

SARA CRAVEN probably had the ideal upbringing for a budding writer. She grew up by the seaside in a house crammed with books, with a box of old clothes to dress up in and a swing outside in a walled garden. She produced the opening of her first book at age five and is eternally grateful to her mother for having kept a straight face. Now she has more than twenty-five novels to her credit. The author is married and has two children.

Books by Sara Craven

HARLEQUIN PRESENTS

Don't miss any of our special offers. Write to us at the following address for information on our newest releases.

Harlequin Reader Service
901 Fuhrmann Blvd., P.O. Box 1397, Buffalo, NY 14240
Canadian address: P.O. Box 603,
Fort Erie, Ont. L2A 5X3

SARA CRAVEN

outsider

Harlequin Books

TORONTO • NEW YORK • LONDON
AMSTERDAM • PARIS • SYDNEY • HAMBURG
STOCKHOLM • ATHENS • TOKYO • MILAN

Harlequin Presents first edition May 1988
Second printing May 1988
ISBN 0-373-11072-3

Original hardcover edition published in 1987
by Mills & Boon Limited

Printed in U.S.A.

CHAPTER ONE

OUTLINED on the hillside against the morning sky, horse and rider looked as if they had been carved from stone. Only the errant breeze, ruffling the mare's mane, and blowing a tress of copper hair across the girl's cheek, revealed that the silhouette was composed of flesh and blood.

Below, in the valley, it was business as usual at the Wintersgarth racing stables. From her eyrie, Natalie Drummond could see the second string going out for exercise. It was a world in miniature, operating as if by clockwork. She drew a swift, satisfied sigh.

My world, she thought. My world as it's never been before.

She would have been down there, riding out with the horses, under normal circumstances, but today she had begged off, told Wes Lovett the head lad to handle the exercising himself. She was too excited, too much on edge to be around highly strung and volatile thorough-breds. Some of her unease would undoubtedly have communicated itself to them, and caused problems.

She ran an affectionate hand down the mare's neck. Whereas dear old Jasmine, of course, was too mature and too equable to care, she thought, smiling, as she glanced at her watch.

It was time she was getting back. They might already have phoned from the clinic to say her father was on his way back, and she wanted to be there when he arrived. It would probably be tactful to change out of her riding gear too, she acknowledged wryly. They would have a leisurely lunch to celebrate the fact that Grantham Slater's heart attack had only been a mild one—a warning shot, Doctor Ellis had called it—and that he was home and safe again, and afterwards, when he was feeling warm and mellow with her stepmother's incredible cooking, she would talk to him about what the consultant had said.

I can do it, she thought, as she turned Jasmine on to the track which led back to the stables. I've proved I can over these past weeks. Grantham can't just dismiss me as an office clerk any more.

Somehow she would make him see that his absurd prejudice about making her his full partner had to be abandoned.

The consultant had been forthright when he'd talked to Beattie and herself. 'He's made an excellent recovery.' He flicked his pen against the blotter on his desk. 'But, inevitably, there are going to have to be some changes in his regimen, changes which he won't like. He's a determined man, and a successful one—a brilliant trainer of steeplechasers, they tell me. Well, I'm not suggesting he retires, but he has to find a way of taking life very much more easily than he has been doing if he wants to avoid a recurrence of his problem.' He looked at Natalie. 'You're his only child, Mrs Drummond?'

She nodded. 'My mother died when I was small. She was expecting another baby, but there were complications.'

'But you do work for your father?'

'Yes, but up to his illness, I was only a secretary. I did the correspondence, manned the phone, and did the book-keeping and accounts.' She looked down at her hands, tightly clasped together in her lap. 'Grantham's rather—old-fashioned. He's never allowed me to be involved in the training side at all. He never even encouraged me to ride—I had to have lessons at school.' She gave a constricted smile. 'But you can't be born and brought up in a racing stable without absorbing a certain amount of expertise. I've managed to put mine to good use while my father's been ill.'

He smiled at her. 'I'm sure you have.' He turned to Beattie. 'And you, Mrs Slater. Are you involved in the running of the stables as well?'

If she hadn't been so worried, Natalie could have collapsed in gales of giggles at the look of sheer horror on Beattie's face. Her stepmother was a warm and lovely lady, but she regarded all horseflesh with acute misgivings, and never went anywhere near the stables if she could help it.

Beattie accompanied her husband to race meetings, knowing that her elegant, expensively clad presence beside him was an affirmation of his prosperity, but she usually stayed away from the paddock.

Now she said weakly, 'I'm afraid not. Do—do you think I should be?'

'I think someone will have to be,' the consultant returned. 'It's essential that your husband starts to share some of his responsibilities.' He looked again at Natalie. 'It would seem, Mrs Drummond, that you're in the ideal position to do this—your family commitments allowing, of course.'

Natalie lifted her chin. 'I'm a widow,' she said quietly. 'Apart from Beattie and my father, I have no family. I'll be glad to do whatever I can to help Grantham.'

'If he'll let you,' Beattie observed frankly as they drove home.

'"If" is right,' Natalie agreed, her fine brows drawing together as she slowed for a traffic light. 'Ever since they allowed him access to a phone, he's been calling Wes with instructions each morning.' She grimaced. 'Fortunately they've invariably been the same instructions that I'd already issued, so Wes just agrees to everything—and on we go.' She sighed. 'One of these days I'll have to tell Grantham I've been running things while he's been away, but I'm not looking forward to it.'

'I don't suppose you are.' Beattie was silent for a moment. 'I've never been able to understand why Grantham keeps you chained to that office desk. Doesn't he realise you have the same feeling for those four-legged monsters that he has himself?'

'He knows.' Natalie let out the clutch and they moved off again. 'I thought at first when he refused point blank to let me work with the horses that it was just plain sexism. He's never employed girls in the stables in any capacity, after all. But it seems to go deeper than that.' She paused. 'I hoped—when I married Tony—that his attitude might soften, but he seemed more determined than ever to keep me out of things. It took me quite a while to realise that he saw in Tony the son he'd always wanted—an heir apparent for Wintersgarth. All I was needed for was to—carry on the succession.'

'Nat, my dear!' There was shock as well as compassion in Beattie's soft voice.

'Do I sound bitter?' Natalie asked ruefully. 'Well, I was, even after Tony was killed. Father seemed to blame me for not being pregnant.' She forced a smile. 'If I'd been a mare, I think he'd have sold me.'

'Or found a better stallion,' said Beattie thoughtfully. Natalie nearly stalled the car.

'Or even that,' she agreed, her voice quivering a little. 'As it is, there's no one left but me, and somehow I have to persuade him to make the best of it, and take me into full partnership. My God, good women trainers aren't exactly unknown in steeplechasing! And I could be good—I know it.' She sighed. 'It isn't my fault I was born female.'

Beattie shot her a dry look. 'Some people might regard it as a distinct advantage.'

'But then you're prejudiced,' Natalie returned affectionately.

The memory of the exchange made her smile as she rode Jasmine sedately under the archway into the stableyard, glancing around her as she did so. Everything as far as she could see had been honed to its usual pristine state. The boxes were gleaming, the gravel had been raked, and there was a busy, excited hum round the place.

All the lads, she knew, were looking forward to seeing her father restored to health, and back where he belonged. Grantham Slater had the reputation of being a hard man in many ways, and an exacting employer, but he was also fair, and paid good wages for good work.

'We know where we stand with the boss,' Wes had once explained it simply to her.

Well, the boss would have nothing to complain of when he did his round at evening stables, as he undoubtedly would, thought Natalie as she rode Jasmine into the second, smaller yard and dismounted.

Beattie was talking optimistically of persuading her husband to take it easy, but Natalie was sure he'd have other ideas.

She led Jasmine into her stall and began to unsaddle her. It had done her good to ride out, helping her to get things into perspective, see how best to tackle her father.

He was a logical man, she thought, as she began to brush Jasmine down. When he realised how well she'd coped in his absence, he'd change his mind about having her as a partner. Besides, what real choice did he have? For once in his life, Grantham Slater would have to bow to circumstance, instead of bending it to his will as he usually did.

'Excuse me, Miss Natalie.' The voice behind her made her jump. She'd been too preoccupied with her own thoughts to hear Ben Watson's approach. 'Mrs Slater's been on the phone, asking for you. I can finish off Jasmine if you want to get up to the house.'

Natalie forced a smile. 'It's all right, I'll see to her myself, thanks.'

Watson lingered. 'I thought you might be in a bit of a hurry. It's a great day, after all.'

She nodded, and concentrated her attention on Jasmine, hoping he would take the hint and go. She'd no idea why she didn't like Ben Watson. He was quiet and polite, and Wes had no complaints about his work, but there was something . . . something about the way he looked at her which had made Natalie wish more than once that she was several inches taller, and a couple of stone heavier, and looked like one of the horses. At the same time, she told herself she was probably imagining things. His attitude to her was always respectful—even deferential.

I've just taken agin him, she thought ruefully, and knew by the sudden slackening of some inner tension that he had departed.

When she got to the house, Beattie was rushing into the dining room with a vase of flowers.

'Would you believe it?' she flung at Natalie. 'Grantham's just rung to say he's invited two extra people to lunch. Bang goes our quiet family party!'

'Oh, Beattie!' Natalie was taken aback. 'That's too bad of him, it really is! Did he say who they were?'

Beattie flapped an agitated hand. 'Well, there's Andrew Bentley, for one—and he did mention the other name, but I've forgotten.' She paused. 'I just hope there's enough food.'

Natalie sent her an affectionate grin. 'Of course there will be. Judging by last night's preparations, you could feed the entire membership of the Jockey Club, if they turned up, let alone Dad's solicitor and some unknown quantity. Is there anything I can do?'

'Not really.' Beattie secretly revelled in domestic crises, her stepdaughter suspected. 'Although—darling, you might put on a dress.'

'I'd already planned to.' Natalie grimaced. 'I don't want to give Dad any cause for complaint, today of all days.'

She was thoughtful as she went up to her room. It seemed odd that Andrew Bentley was coming to lunch on Grantham's first day out of the clinic. Was he coming as legal adviser, or family friend? she wondered. If it was purely a social visit, then Liz would probably be coming with him, and that would explain the extra person. But that can't be, she thought rather restively. Beattie and Liz are friends. She wouldn't forget the name of Andrew's wife, no matter how much of a flap she was in.

She showered swiftly, then dressed in a simple navy shirtwaister—a compromise, she thought as she tugged a comb through her tangle of copper hair, between the ultra-feminine clothes Grantham preferred her to wear, and the businesslike exterior she wished to present. She toyed with the idea of putting her hair up, but decided that would be carrying the new efficient image too far.

Excitement always made her pale, so she added a judicious amount of blusher to her cheeks, and a modicum of shadow to emphasise the lustre of her green eyes under their sweep of dark lashes.

Daddy's pretty little daughter, she thought with irony as she surveyed the results of her labours. Only not a cipher any more, but a force to be reckoned with.

She heard the sound of a car on the drive, and flew to the window. It was the hired vehicle Grantham had insisted on, having explosively turned down his wife and daughter's offers to drive him home themselves.

'Women drivers!' he'd snorted. 'I'm not in line for another heart attack, thank you!'

'Chauvinist,' Beattie had teased, squeezing his hand with love, but Natalie found her own smile rather fixed.

Now she hung back a little, waiting for her father and his wife to enjoy their reunion in a certain amount of privacy. Or was that an excuse, because the thought of facing Grantham on his own ground was suddenly a daunting one?

Natalie squared her shoulders and went downstairs.

Grantham was ensconced in his favourite chair in the drawing room. He was a big man still, although he had lost weight since his illness. Here and there in his thick grey thatch of hair, a few streaks of copper like Natalie's own still lingered. He had a strong face which could look harsh, but was now relaxed in the pleasure of seeing his home, and his wife again. His smile widened for Natalie.

'Well, my girl?'

'Very well, thanks.' She stooped and kissed him. 'And you look fine yourself.'

He gave her a derisive look. 'A dramatic improvement on last night, eh?'

'A dramatic improvement every day from now on,' she told him steadily. 'As long...'

'As long as I do what the doctor tells me,' he finished for her, his tone quite amiable. 'Well, I intend to, lass, I intend to. I've had a shock, and I don't mind admitting it. I didn't think it would happen to me. So there'll have to be some changes.' He gave her an enigmatic look. 'And they'll involve you.'

Natalie's heart skipped a beat, but she kept her voice level. No girlish excitement, she told herself fiercely, and no grovelling gratitude either. I've worked for this moment, and I've deserved it. 'I thought perhaps we might talk after lunch,' she said.

'I can say what I've got to say now.' He paused. 'I suppose Beattie told you I've asked Andrew to lunch.'

'Yes, she did.' Natalie ruffled his hair. 'Bit of a dirty trick, landing her with last-minute guests.'

'She can manage,' said Grantham calmly. 'And I wanted to get things settled—put on a proper footing without delay. Owners are queer folk. They don't like uncertainty.'

Don't I know it! Natalie said silently. The hours I've spent on the phone reassuring a whole list of them that it's business as usual, and that there's no need to take their horses away so close to the start of the jumping season.

Aloud, she said, 'There haven't been any real problems.'

'I should think not,' he said with a touch of his old asperity. 'They know when they're well off, most of them. I train winners in this yard, not also-bloody-rans.' He glanced at his watch. 'Where's Andrew? I told him

to be here by twelve. It's these damned motorways—
they're always digging them up.'

Natalie's brows shot up. 'But Andrew doesn't have to
use the motorway,' she pointed out mildly. 'He's coming
from Harrogate.'

'I know he is. It's t'other one, driving up from Lambourn. Andrew's bringing him here.' Grantham's tone
was short.

'From Lambourn?' echoed Natalie, frowning. 'Who
in the world's coming all that distance?'

'Eliot Lang.'

'Good God,' Natalie said slowly. 'The playboy of
National Hunt racing, no less! And why is he venturing
this far north?' Her eyes widened. 'Is he going to ride
for us?'

Grantham snorted. 'Of course not. He's retired. It was
all over the papers two months since.'

She remembered now. It had caused quite a sensation—one of the country's top steeplechase riders and
a former champion jockey retiring in his early thirties.
She'd absorbed the information and then discarded it as
having no significance to her.

Now, suddenly, she wasn't so sure.

She said, 'Then what is he coming for?'

'He's coming because I've asked him to,' said her
father. 'It isn't a decision I've made lightly. If I were
still on my own in life, I'd probably have said hang the
doctors, and carried on as usual. But there's Beattie to
think of now.' His face softened. 'We've only been
married two years, and I don't reckon on making her a
widow quite yet, so I'm going to behave myself, and
take the advice I've been given as if I was grateful for
it—which I'm not. These are my stables, and I built them
up from what your grandfather left, and I'd no thought

to share them with anyone except my own kith and kin. But with Tony gone, and no grandchild to think of, I had to reconsider. And they tell me I need a partner to take the weight of this place off my shoulders.'

Natalie knew what was coming, and was terrified by it. She said urgently, 'Dad, I could...'

'That you couldn't.' One brief phrase smashed her dreams to smithereens. 'You know my views, and they haven't changed. I need a man—someone who knows jump racing, and can stand shoulder to shoulder with me. Lang's never ridden for me, but I've always respected him, even if he did get his name into the gossip columns more than I care for. Well, a lad must sow his wild oats, I suppose. Anyway, the papers said he was thinking of going into training, so I got Andrew to contact him, and we've agreed terms. He's buying a half share in Wintersgarth.'

She felt numb. There was a fold of her dress between her fingers, and she was pleating and unpleating it endlessly as she tried to assimilate what he had been saying.

The weeks of struggle, of trying to prove herself, had all been in vain. While she'd been working her guts out through all the hours God sent to keep Wintersgarth together, Grantham had been making his own plans. Plans which totally excluded her, she realised.

She ran the tip of her tongue round dry lips. 'And what's going to happen to me?'

Her father looked at her as if the question surprised him. 'Well, you'll do your normal job, same as always. He's quite amenable to that.'

She said thickly, 'How good—how very good of him.'

'And you'll be provided for in the long term, naturally, if there's need.'

If there was need ... Natalie's head reeled. All her life she'd been totally dependent on her father. At school, she'd opted for a commercial course rather than pursue an academic career so that she could work in the stables office. Because in those days, naïvely, she'd thought that might be a foot in the door to better things.

And marriage had changed nothing. She had met Tony shortly after her father had employed him as stable jockey on a retainer, and the wedding had taken place two months later, which meant there were two of them dependent on Grantham Slater instead of one. Tony had been a more than promising jockey, and he had enjoyed the fruits of his success, living for the present. After he had been killed, she discovered he'd been living on overdraft. She had paid it off, but the way the debts had been incurred still rankled ... She closed her mind abruptly, and focused on what was happening here in this room, right now.

'I suppose I must be grateful for small mercies. At least I still have a roof over my head.'

'There's no need to take that tone.' His voice was repressive. 'And don't tell me you'd thoughts of filling my shoes here, because I know it already. And you know my opinion on the subject. Or did you think a heart attack would soften my brain as well? The stables are no place for you, Natalie. They never were, and they never will be, so make your mind up to it. And keep off the backs of my thoroughbreds,' he added. 'A time or two I phoned here to be told you were out with one of the strings. That stops as of now, although I won't deny you the exercise you need. Maybe old Jasmine's bit tame for you. I'll find you a good hack ...'

'No, thanks.' Natalie shook her head. 'Jasmine suits me very well.'

An hour ago, barely more, she had sat on that hill with the world at her feet. Now, everything she had ever wanted had been snatched away from her and given to a stranger, although that was surely a misnomer applied to Eliot Lang. His career and lifestyle had been described so often in the newspapers as to make them totally fam-iliar.

Unlike Tony, who had been an apprentice, Eliot Lang had started his racing career as an amateur. He'd enjoyed a meteoric success, which hadn't prevented his wealthy family protesting volubly when he became a professional. And he had been making headlines ever since. He'd spent several seasons riding for Kevin Laidlaw, and then had left in a blaze of publicity and innuendo which said that Laidlaw had dismissed him because he couldn't keep his hands off his wife. The Laidlaws had vehemently denied the rumours, but Eliot Lang had said 'No comment' and gone to ride for Duncan Sanders, who was divorced. At least from then on he'd seemed to keep away from married women, perhaps because of the horsewhipping Kevin Laidlaw was alleged to have threated him with. But he had never maintained a low profile. The good life was there, and he enjoyed it, in the company of a succession of models and actresses, few of them distinguishable from their predecessors. And at the same time, he took more winners past the post than his rivals thought decent. His cottage in Lambourn had been the subject of a colour spread in a Sunday supplement.

Her mouth curling in distaste, Natalie thought, He'll find Wintersgarth dull.

Aloud she asked, 'Does Beattie know what you intend?'

She was thankful when her father shook his head. If Beattie had known, and not told her, that would have been another betrayal, and she felt bruised enough.

She got to her feet. 'I'll go and see if we've got any of Andrew's favourite sherry.'

'That's a good lass.'

That was what he approved of, she thought bitterly as she went out into the hall—her ability to deal with small domestic details, to shelter him from unwanted phone calls from querulous owners.

In the kitchen, Beattie was stirring a pan of soup on the Aga. She said over a shoulder, 'Have a look at the dining-room, and tell me if it's all right.' Then she saw Natalie's white face and blazing eyes, and her tone sharpened. 'Nat darling, whatever's the matter?'

'Eliot Lang,' said Natalie. 'The man whose name you forgot.'

'Why, so it is.' Beattie shook her head. 'I knew it was something familiar. He's some kind of jockey, isn't he?'

'He certainly was,' Natalie said grittily. 'Now he's going to be some kind of trainer—here.'

Beattie's lips parted in a soundless gasp, then she turned back to her soup. There was a prolonged silence, then she said, 'But where does that leave you?'

'Back at square one, where I apparently belong. Only I now have two bosses.'

Beattie said half to herself, 'He told me he had a surprise, but it never occurred to me...' She stopped. 'Oh, my dear child, I'm so sorry! It's so cruel—so unnecessary.'

'So unacceptable,' Natalie completed. 'If I'm going to be a dogsbody, I can find another office somewhere—preferably as far from racing as possible.'

Beattie transferred her pan to the simmering plate. She said, 'You don't mean that.'

'Oh, but I do,' Natalie said bitterly. 'I've had enough. I've tried my damnedest for Dad, but I'm never going to measure up to the standard he wants—because I don't even know what his criteria are, and I suspect he doesn't either.'

'All the same,' said Beattie, 'you mustn't leave.'

'You think I'd stay and watch that—that racetrack Romeo help himself to my inheritance?' Natalie asked fiercely. 'Over my dead body!'

Beattie said quietly, 'If you leave now, like this, it could be over Grantham's.' She sat down beside Natalie at the kitchen table. 'We're not supposed to expose him to any kind of upset—the doctor said so.'

'He probably wouldn't even notice I'd gone—until he wanted his letters typed, or found the owners weren't paying their bills on time.'

'That isn't true, and you know it,' Beattie said roundly. 'He loves you, Nat, although I admit he has a very strange way of showing it. He has this—fixation about women working with horses.' She paused. 'I think one of the reasons he fell in love with me is that I know nothing about the beasts except that they bite at one end, and kick at the other.' She smiled at Natalie. 'There were a lot of women after him, you know, who had strong connections with racing, who'd have been able to talk to him about horses in an intelligent manner. Coral LeFevre, for one.'

In spite of her wretchedness, Natalie felt her lips curve in the ghost of a smile. 'The Black Widow? What makes you think that?'

'The way she still looks at him,' said Beattie simply. 'I know that a lot of your father's friends and colleagues were horrified when he married me, when there were so many more suitable wives around.' She thought for a minute. 'But my attraction for your father was my *unsuitability*, somehow. We met at a concert he'd been dragged to, and he didn't mind that I thought the Derby and the Grand National were the same kind of race. He's never minded it. In a way, I'm part of the same fixation. I'm happy with my music and my cooking, and that makes Grantham happy too. I can't explain it.' She gave Natalie a level look. 'I sympathise with you, every step of the way, but I love Grantham, and I won't have him upset for any reason, however good. If you really want to leave, wait a few weeks until he's stronger, and feelings have cooled. You can't quarrel with him, Nat. I won't allow it.'

There was a long silence, then Natalie said dully, 'Very well. You're right, of course. I'd never forgive myself if there was a row, and it caused—problems.' She shook herself, and stood up. 'But I can't sit at that table with Eliot Lang and eat lunch as if nothing has happened. Make some excuse for me, Beattie, please. Tell them I've got a headache, or bubonic plague, or something.'

Beattie groaned. 'I'll do my best—but, Nat, your father won't be pleased.'

Natalie opened the kitchen door. She said, 'I promise you he'd be even less pleased to hear me tell Eliot Lang to go to hell.'

That, she thought, was relatively mild compared with what she'd really like to say to him, so why was Beattie sitting there looking as if she'd been frozen?

She turned to walk into the hall, and cannoned straight into six foot of bone, sinew and muscle, standing there on the threshold. As unusually strong arms steadied her, she thought confusedly, Andrew? and realised in the same moment that it couldn't be. Andrew was only medium height and distinctly pudgy. Whereas this man, she thought as she took a hurried step backwards, hadn't a spare ounce of flesh anywhere.

Her face burning, she looked up to encounter hazel eyes regarding her with no expression whatever.

'Now, why should you tell me any such thing?' said Eliot Lang.

CHAPTER TWO

NATALIE wanted the floor to open and swallow her, but it remained disappointingly solid, so she rallied her defences.

'I think that's my business,' she retorted, her chin tilted dangerously. 'Perhaps you should remember what they say about eavesdroppers, Mr Lang,' She realised his hands were still gripping her upper arms, not too gently, and she stiffened. 'And will you kindly get your hands off me!'

He released her so promptly it was almost an insult. Then he was walking past her, the thin, tanned face relaxing into a smile.

'Mrs Slater?' He held out his hand to Beattie. 'I'm sorry for this apparent intrusion, but your husband thought you might not have heard Mr Bentley's car arrive, so I volunteered to find you.' He looked round him, his smile widening. 'Not that it's any hardship,' he added appreciatively. 'Something smells absolutely fantastic!'

'It's just ordinary home cooking,' said Beattie with modest untruthfulness, as she shook hands with him. Her candid grey eyes looked him over. 'You look as if you could do with some.'

He laughed. 'You could be right. I've spent so many years living on starvation rations to keep my weight down, that it's hard to believe I can now eat as much as I want.'

There was a pause, then Beattie said with slight awkwardness, 'And this, of course, is my stepdaughter Natalie.'

He turned back towards Natalie. 'How do you do,' he said with cool civility.

The swift charm which had bowled over Beattie, it seemed, could be switched on and off at will, Natalie thought with contempt.

She returned a mechanically conventional greeting, then excused herself on the grounds that she had to see to the drinks.

Her retreat was in good order, but when she was safely alone, she found her heart was pounding as if she'd taken to her heels and fled from him.

It was infuriating to realise she had been betrayed into such a schoolgirlish piece of rudeness, but at least Eliot Lang now knew quite unequivocally where he stood where she was concerned, she thought defiantly.

Andrew's greeting was rather less ebullient then usual, she realised as she took the drinks into the drawing-room. He knew, none better, how desperately keen she'd been to join Grantham as his partner, and she thought she saw a measure of compassion in his gaze, as he swapped genialities with her about how good it was to have her father back again, and how well he was looking.

Gradually she recovered her composure, and by the time Eliot Lang accompanied her stepmother into the room, she was able to meet the rather searching look he sent her with an appearance, at least, of indifference.

She found, to her annoyance, that she was stationed opposite him at the dining-table, although the conversation was general enough to enable her to avoid having to address him directly. Her father was in his most expansive and relaxed mood, making no secret of his delight at the success of his plans.

Naturally, as the meal wore on, the talk turned to racing, and Eliot Lang's past triumphs, although in fairness Natalie had to admit the subject wasn't introduced by him, and he seemed reluctant to discuss them, commenting instead with open wryness on his failure ever to ride a Grand National winner.

'It's only one race,' Grantham leaned back in his chair. 'And that last Gold Cup of yours must have made up for everything.'

Eliot Lang laughed. He had good teeth, Natalie noticed, white and very even. 'It was Storm Trooper's race. All I had to do was sit tight.'

'Don't denigrate yourself, lad. He nearly went at that last fence, thanks to that damned loose horse. You held him up, and took him on.' Grantham shook his head. 'A great win—a truly great win.'

Natalie stole a covert look at Eliot Lang under her lashes, trying to visualise him sweat-streaked and mud-splashed. In the dark, elegant suit, its waistcoat accentuating his slim waist, the gleam of a silk tie setting off his immaculate white shirt, he looked more like a successful City executive.

And he was undeniably attractive, she thought resentfully, if you liked that sort of thing, his good looks only slightly marred by the slanting scar that slashed across one cheekbone.

It was a tough face, the cleft in his chin, and the firm line of his mouth emphasising the ruthlessness and determination which had always been a hallmark of his riding. 'Fearless', she recalled unwillingly, had been one of the adjectives most often used by the sports writers.

With a faint shock, she realised he was watching her in his turn, a faintly cynical smile playing round his lips. Natalie transferred her gaze hastily back to her plate, trying to control her confusion.

He probably thought she was another potential conquest, she thought scornfully. Well, he would soon discover his mistake.

Beattie was speaking. 'After all the success and the excitement, Mr Lang, aren't you going to find training rather—mundane?'

He smiled at her. 'Won't you please call me Eliot? And the simple answer to your question is—no, I'm sure I won't. I'm looking forward immensely to joining you here at Wintersgarth.'

'But you're still quite young to have retired from National Hunt racing,' persisted Beattie. 'Grantham says you still had years of winning in front of you.'

He shrugged ironically, 'Perhaps.'

'So how could you bear to turn your back on it, when you were still at the peak?'

He was silent for a moment, the straight dark brows drawn together. 'I suppose it was a question of motivation,' he said at last. 'I had a couple of bad falls last season.' His hand went up and touched the scar. 'They rather brought home to me that I was over thirty now, and that letting horses stamp you into the mud was not the way I wanted to spend part of the next decade. I had to start thinking about a new career, and as I want to stay with horses, training seemed the ideal answer.' He smiled. 'Once I'd made up my mind, it really wasn't that hard to walk away.'

Natalie said, 'And will you find it just as easy to walk away from us when you've had enough?'

His brows lifted. 'This isn't a whim, Miss Slater. It's strictly business. I'm investing in Wintersgarth.'

'I'm sure we're all very grateful,' she said. 'Not that we need your money—we've always made out financially. But it's natural I should be concerned about your—er—motivation. After all, you don't exactly have a reputation for fidelity.'

'Natalie!' It was a bark from her father, his face thunderous. He turned to Eliot. 'I must apologise for my daughter. Sometimes her tongue runs away with her.'

'On the contrary,' said Eliot, 'If she has misgivings, it's best that they're aired now.' He leaned across the table, his hazel eyes boring into Natalie's. 'My partnership with your father isn't just a flash in the pan, Miss Slater. I'm coming to him to learn from his genius, and maybe contribute some skills of my own, and it's for the rest of my life.' He added drily, 'I'm sorry if that doesn't fit the image you seem to have of me.'

She was furiously aware she'd been cut down to size by an expert.

She said, 'That's—reassuring. But you live in the South. Your life has been based there, near the bright lights. Aren't you going to find Yorkshire quiet and dull?'

'Even the brightest lights can pall.' He looked amused. 'And I was born here, you know, although admittedly it was more by accident than design. My parents were staying with friends during the hunting season, and had totally misjudged the possible time of my arrival.'

Everyone was laughing with him, enjoying the slackening of tension, although the glance Grantham bestowed on Natalie was minatory, promising a tongue-lashing later.

She wished now she'd kept quiet. There was obviously nothing to be gained from confrontation.

'What will you do about your lovely cottage?' Beattie asked. 'Keep it for weekends?'

'No.' Eliot shook his head. 'I've already told one of the local agents to put it on his books.' He paused. 'But you're not going to be lumbered with a lodger, Mrs Slater. I'm quite self-sufficient, I promise you, and your husband mentioned something about a self-contained flat over the garages that might be suitable, at least on a temporary basis.'

Natalie said sharply, 'The flat? Dad, you didn't!'

Grantham's florid face adopted a moderately apologetic expression. 'Maybe I should have talked it over with you, lass, but I've had other things on my mind.' He turned to Eliot. 'My daughter's name is Drummond, actually. She was widowed three years ago, but the flat in question was built to accommodate Nat and her husband originally.'

Eliot's eyes surveyed Natalie's bare hands briefly, then he said, 'I'm sorry, I didn't realise. Naturally if it's going to cause Mrs Drummond any distress, I'll willingly look for an alternative.'

'Nonsense,' Grantham said robustly. 'The flat's there, and it's empty. Nat never goes near the place. Anyway, have a look at it, and see what you think.'

Natalie didn't want to hear any more. She pushed back her chair and stood up. 'I won't have coffee, Beattie. I have to telephone the feed merchant.' She sketched some kind of smile round the table. 'If you'll excuse me...?'

The office was a big, cluttered comfortable room, and it seemed like a sanctuary to Natalie as she sank into the chair behind her desk. She had letters to reply to, messages on the answering machine to listen to, as well as the call to the feed merchant, but for a moment she could deal with none of it. The thought of Eliot Lang taking over the home where her marriage to Tony had started out with such high hopes sickened her. Although she might have felt differently if she'd liked him, she admitted, biting her lip. Or would she?

When she had moved out, to resume life in her old room in her father's house after the funeral, she'd turned the key in the lock as if she was closing off a part of her life. It had never occurred to her that it might have to be re-opened. They had never needed the flat. The lads had their own block, and Wes had a cottage in the village.

She supposed she should have seen it coming, but she hadn't . . .

She shivered, then drew the phone towards her and began to dial the feed merchant's number. In deference to Beattie's wishes, she would carry on here until Grantham's health was assured, but then she would be off and running, she told herself grimly. And she would start looking round to see what jobs were available without delay. Grantham would find he was not the only one who could hold his cards close to his chest.

Her father came into the office half an hour later. She had half expected Andrew and Eliot Lang to be with him, but he was alone. He walked past her into the inner office, which was far smaller, and more luxuriously appointed, and which he kept for entertaining favoured owners.

'Come through, will you,' he said over his shoulder, as he disappeared through the door.

Oh, hell, Natalie thought, as she rose to her feet. Now I'm for it! And I swore I wouldn't upset him.

She picked up the ledgers, and carried them through with her. She said meekly, 'I thought you might like to see the accounts, Dad.'

'All in good time,' he returned. He reached for the big silver cigar box, drew it towards him, then with a resigned air pushed it away again. 'I feel undressed without them, damn it,' he muttered, then focused sharply on his daughter. He said grimly, 'Disappointment is one thing, Natalie, although it's fair to say you built your own hopes up. I never did. But bloody rudeness and cussedness is another, and it has to stop. Do I make myself clear?' He paused. 'I was at fault over the flat business, and I admit it, although I didn't know you had any sentimental attachment to it. But it's standing empty, and I'm paying rates on it, so it might as well be let or sold. And there's no reason why Eliot shouldn't use it while he looks for his own place. Is there?'

He waited, while she shook her head, slowly and reluctantly.

'That's settled then.' he leaned back in his chair. 'Eliot's joining us here, Natalie, whether you like it or not, my girl. We signed the papers after lunch, so you're going to have to make the best of it, and if you've any sense, you'll get on with him.' He gave her a dry look. 'A lot of lasses seem to take to him. No reason why you can't too, even if he has put your nose out of joint.'

'Do you really think it's that simple?' she asked bitterly.

'I think you're making difficulties where there are none,' he retorted calmly. 'I'll tell you something. Eliot's more than ready to meet you half-way. He'd probably be glad of some company—someone to show him the countryside round here.'

Her lips parted in disbelief as she looked down at him. 'You're not serious?'

'I'm not joking either.' He shook his head. 'You've been living like a nun for the past three years, Natalie, and don't tell me any different. But you can't grieve for ever, lass, so why not get out a bit—live a little?' He smiled. 'You never know, you might...'

'No!' Natalie exploded. 'Oh, I know what you're thinking, and if wasn't so nauseating, it would be ridiculous. Your first attempt at matchmaking worked, so be content with that. There'll never be another. Eliot Lang is the last kind of man I'd ever want to be involved with. His—type revolts me. If he ever touched me—I'd die!' She stopped with a little gasp, looking anxiously at her father, but he seemed perfectly composed.

'Well, if that's how you feel, I'll say no more.' He picked up a paperweight carved in the shape of a horse, and began to toy with it. 'But there's no accounting for taste, I must say. He's got my Beattie eating out of his hand already,' he added with a faint grin. 'But you're going to be civil to Eliot, and you can start by showing him round the yard—and the flat.'

'Is that an order?' she asked huskily.

'If it needs to be,' he said genially. 'Now, off you go.'

Eliot was waiting by the tack room. Leaning against the door, his hands in his pockets, enjoying the warmth of the afternoon sun, he looked relaxed and very much at home.

'Ah,' he said lazily. 'My guide.' He looked at the bunch of keys dangling from her hand. 'Shall we have a look at the flat first?'

She was taken aback. 'But don't you want to see the yard—the horses?'

'I've done my homework,' he said drily. 'I know what horses are in training here, what they cost, and what the next season's hopes are. Any more I want to know on that score, I can ask Wes Lovett, when he comes back for evening stables. I don't want to intrude on his time with his family.'

'I can tell you anything you want to know.'

'All right,' he said. 'Tell me, Mrs Drummond, what makes you tick. And why I'm so clearly not the flavour of the month.'

Natalie looked past him, remembering Grantham's strictures, and measuring her words accordingly.

She said abruptly, 'You were—a shock. I had no idea Grantham was planning to take on an outsider as a partner.'

'Then what did you think he'd do? Carry on as if nothing had happened? As if that attack had been a figment of his imagination?'

The note in his voice stung her, and she flushed. 'No, of course not. But there was an alternative.'

'What was that?' he asked. 'As a matter of academic interest, of course.'

She said baldly, and ungrammatically, 'There was me.'

There was a long silence. Then Eliot said, 'Everything suddenly becomes much clearer. Well, well. So you see yourself as a trainer of champion 'chasers, do you, Mrs Drummond?'

'Yes, I do. For years I've been begging my father to give me a chance ever since I left school. When he was ill, I thought it was an opportunity to show him that I wasn't—a useless female, but prove I could run things here.'

'I see.' He gave her a meditative look. 'I'm glad to hear natural concern for his well-being wasn't allowed to stand in the way of your ambition.'

Her voice shook. 'You're deliberately misunderstanding me. Of course I was worried—worried sick. But

it wouldn't have improved Grantham's chances of recovery if I'd simply—sat back and let the yard go to
pot.'

He nodded. 'And on the strength of that, you expected
to be made a partner in equal standing with your father
in these stables.' He gave her a long look. 'Lady, you're
living in a dream world. You should know, none better,
just how many million pounds you have on the hoof in
this place. Do you imagine, in the long run, the owners
are going to entrust their treasures to the care of an inexperienced girl, however eager to learn? How old are
you, by the way?'

'I'm twenty-three,' Natalie said stormily. 'And you
couldn't be more wrong. When Dad was first taken ill,
a number of the owners got edgy and started talking
about removing their horses, and I talked them out of
it. I persuaded them I knew what I was doing. So some
people were prepared to have faith in me, even if you
and Grantham want to—shut me out.'

He said quietly, 'Calm down, Mrs Drummond, and
take a firm grip on yourself, because I'm afraid I'm going
to have to shatter another illusion. No amount of sweet-
talking from you kept those horses here. Grantham gave
me a list of those most likely to waver, and I made it
my business to ring them, and tell them what was in the
wind. That was what convinced them, darling. Not your
well-meaning intervention.'

She tried to speak, to say something, but no words
would come. At last she said hoarsely, 'I don't believe
you.'

He shrugged. 'As you wish, but Grantham will
confirm what I say.'

There was a pause, then he added more gently, 'But there's no question of wanting to shut you out, on my part at least. Now, shall we take a look at the flat?'

Natalie felt humiliated to her very soul as she walked in front of him. If her attitude to Eliot had wounded his delicate male pride, then he'd had his revenge in full, she thought wretchedly. At the time, she had thought it was next to a miracle when one owner after another had phoned her back to say that perhaps they'd been hasty...

The flat entrance lay round to the side of the big garage block. Natalie unlocked the front door and stood back. 'I'll wait here,' she said.

Eliot gave her a wry look, seemed as if he was about to speak, then thought better of it, and went up the internal staircase.

Natalie knew an ignominious urge to run away and hide somewhere, while his back was turned. He'd robbed her of everything now, not just the partnership which she recognised would probably never have been hers anyway, but also of her pride in what she had considered her achievements while Grantham was ill.

Oh, it had been cruel of him! Cruel, she thought, her teeth savaging the soft inner flesh of her lower lip. 'Cruel to be kind' was one of Grantham's favourite maxims. Clearly Eliot Lang belonged to the same school of thought.

He was gone a long time. She was thankful that everything had been removed, every stick of furniture, every ornament and keepsake. She would have loathed the idea of him touching her things, using her chairs and table— her bed.

The thought struck her like a blow, her mind flinching from the images it presented, reviving memories she'd thought were dormant.

Tony, she thought wretchedly. Oh God—Tony!

Footsteps coming down the stairs gave sufficient warning for her to compose herself before Eliot rejoined her.

He said flatly, 'You don't leave many clues. That place is totally—empty.' He sent her a narrow-eyed stare. 'Are you Tony Drummond's widow?'

'Yes, what of it?'

He shrugged, still staring at her. 'I should have made the connection before,' he said, half to himself.

'Are you—going to live there?' She had to know.

'Oh, yes, I think so,' he said almost casually. 'As I'm clearly not desecrating some private shrine. And it's big enough to take some of the furniture I want to bring up from Lambourn.'

'Good,' she said. 'Then everyone's happy.'

'A slight exaggeration, wouldn't you say?' he drawled. 'Now I'd like to see the kind of accommodation the lads use. Is that possible?'

'Of course,' Natalie said ironically. 'You're the boss, after all.'

Eliot Lang shot her a sideways glance, but made no reply.

He was silent too as she showed him the block Grantham had built a few years before, with its big kitchen and recreation area on the ground floor, leading up to small, economically fitted single bedrooms upstairs.

'Each room has a handbasin, but there's a communal shower block at the end,' Natalie told him, niggled that he wasn't more openly impressed.

'Just showers?' he asked. 'No bathrooms?'

'Yes, there are two, leading off the shower room.'

'Do they lock?'

Natalie shrugged. 'I suppose so. Is it important?'

'I think privacy can be very important. The bedrooms all have locks, I see.'

'Yes, and they can be opened from the outside by a master key in case someone's taken ill.' Natalie stared at him. 'Why this obsession with locks and bolts?'

'I'm thinking of offering someone a job,' he said shortly. 'So I want to make sure certain standards are observed.'

'My God!' she exclaimed derisively, 'What are they used to—the Hilton? Let me tell you my father spent a fortune on this block, and it's regarded as a model.'

'Oh, I've no real criticism to make. All too often lads are allowed to shift as best they can while the horses get the five-star treatment.'

'You don't approve of that either?' she demanded tartly.

'I think there's reason in all things,' he returned.

She glanced at her watch. 'Perhaps we should move on. The lads usually go down to the snooker club in the village this afternoon, and they'll be back shortly. With your passion for privacy, you'll understand they may not care to find us snooping round their sleeping quarters.'

His mouth twisted slightly. 'Then let's go on with the tour.'

'You mean you're actually going to let me tell you about the horses?' she marvelled. 'I'm honoured!' She paused, a small frown puckering her brow. 'But I don't usually go into the yard empty-handed.'

'We won't today,' he said. 'I begged some carrots from your stepmother. I left them in the tack room.'

As they walked back under the arch, Natalie was bitterly conscious of Eliot's presence beside her, looming over her, a shadow in her personal sun. He must have gone very hungry a lot of the time to keep his weight to a reasonable level for his height, she thought vindictively.

She hated the way he looked around him as they walked along. It was—proprietorial, as if he'd already taken charge.

Well, he could be in for a shock. He was only the junior partner, and he would find, unless she missed her guess, that Grantham had every intention of remaining firmly in the saddle.

Eliot said, as if he'd broken in somehow on her thoughts, 'Your father has made quite a name for himself in schooling difficult horses.'

'Yes,' she agreed. 'He's fantastic with them.'

'I'm sure he is,' he said. 'What a pity one can't apply the same techniques to difficult women.'

He opened the tack room door and motioned her ahead of him with a faintly mocking gesture. He was smiling.

But not for long, she thought.

'Tell me, Mr Lang,' she said, poisonously sweet, 'are those teeth your own?'

'Indeed they are, Mrs Drummond,' he said gravely. 'Would you like me to prove it by biting you?'

She saw the bag of carrots on a shelf, and was glad of an excuse to move away from him. 'No, I wouldn't.'

'What a pity,' he said. 'Because it's time someone made a mark on you, sweetheart.' He'd followed her, and as she reached for the carrots, he took her by the shoulders and turned her to face him, picking up her slim, ringless left hand and studying it, brows raised. 'Because the unfortunate Tony doesn't seem to have left much of an impression, in any way.'

Outraged, Natalie tried to pull away from his grasp. 'Let go of me!'

'Why?' he jeered. 'Because you'll die if I touch you?'
He mimicked a falsetto, and smiled cynically as her lips
parted in a soundless gasp. 'Well, let's risk it and see.'

She tried to say 'No', but her protest was stifled as
his mouth descended on hers. He was thorough, and not
particularly gentle. All the antagonism between them was
there in the kiss, but charged, explosive with some other
element she could neither recognise nor analyse.

When at last Eliot released her, flushed and breathless,
she took a step backwards, leaning against a cupboard,
aware that her legs were trembling so much she was in
real danger of collapsing on the floor.

Eliot's hand reached out, half cupping her breast, his
fingers seeking the place where her heart hammered unevenly against her ribs.

'You see?' he said drily. 'You survived, after all.'

Was this survival, Natalie thought dazedly, this crip-
pling confusion of mind and body? This strange quivering ache deep inside that she had never known before?
And all this for a kiss that hadn't been a kiss at all, but
some kind of punishment.

Mutely she stared up at him, seeing the mockery fade
suddenly from the hazel eyes, watching them grow curiously intent as his hand moved with new purpose on
the swell of her breast, his fingers seeking the tumescent
nipple through the thin dark blue cotton of her dress.

And was as suddenly removed. He said, 'I think we
have company.'

In a disconnected part of her mind, Natalie heard the
sound of voices, the crunch of boots on gravel. Wes,
she thought, and the others coming back for evening
stables.

Eliot reached past her and retrieved the bag of carrots.
His arm brushed against her, and her body went rigid.

He was aware of the reaction, and smiled sardonically down into her white face.

'A piece of advice, Mrs Drummond,' he said lightly. 'In future when you want to slag me off, keep your voice down—unless you want to suffer the consequences.'

He walked away, leaving her still leaning against the cupboard as if she had neither the strength nor the will to move.

CHAPTER THREE

As SOON as she had pulled herself together, Natalie went up to the house and straight to her room, bypassing Beattie who could be heard humming happily to herself in the kitchen.

And in her room she stayed, until a couple of hours later Andrew's Jaguar pulled away, with his passenger safely on board.

When she ventured downstairs, Beattie was alone in the drawing-room, sipping a sherry, and putting a few stitches in a piece of embroidery with an air of satisfaction that was almost tangible.

'I've persuaded your father to have a rest before dinner,' she told Natalie happily. 'I asked Andrew and Eliot to stay, but they had to get back.' Her eyes twinkled, and she lowered her voice conspiratorially. 'Andrew told me that Eliot didn't travel up here alone. Apparently he has a lady companion, booked into the International Hotel.' She pursed her lips with mock primness. 'Blonde hair, apparently, and a figure like a Page Three girl. I think Andrew was quite envious, poor old thing!'

Natalie forced a smile, as she poured herself a drink. 'I suppose voluptuous blondes are going to become part of the scenery from now on.' She tried to speak lightly, but the words sounded stilted, but fortunately Beattie seemed unaware.

'One thing's certain,' she said. 'Nothing will ever be the same round here.'

To Natalie, the words sounded like a prophecy of doom.

That night, as she was brushing her hair, she found she was studying herself in the mirror, almost clinically. Her face, naturally pale under the cloud of copper hair, was like a small cat's with its green eyes and high cheekbones. Not the face of a woman at peace with herself, but there was little wonder about that. For the rest of her—medium height with a figure on the thin side of slender.

About as far removed from a Page Three girl as it was possible to get, she told herself in bitter self-derision. And as that was where Eliot's tastes lay, that would seem to guarantee her immunity in the future as long as she behaved herself.

He had things to settle in Lambourn, so he wouldn't be returning to Yorkshire immediately, which would give her a breathing space to come to terms with the change at Wintersgarth.

He had commissioned Beattie to engage a local decorating firm to repaint the flat, and would be sending up a list of the exact colours he wanted on the walls. The quiet neutrals she had chosen were being banished for ever, it seemed.

Over dinner, listening to Grantham and Beattie discussing their immediate plans, Natalie had broken in abruptly.

'Did you know he might be bringing some extra staff with him?'

'He mentioned it, yes,' Grantham nodded.

'You didn't mention we were up to strength?'

He smiled broadly, 'At the moment, lass, maybe. But an extra pair of hands won't hurt—and there'll be more horses to see to.'

'Oh, of course,' she said, heavily sarcastic. 'We're going to be deluged with owners wanting us to take their horses now that the great Eliot Lang is coming amongst us. No doubt he told you so himself.'

'He's had a couple of approaches from people he's ridden for,' Grantham said mildly. 'What's odd about that?'

She bit her lip. 'Approaches are one thing, firm offers are another.' She looked at him anxiously. 'Dad, don't go overboard, will you?'

He shook his head. 'I had a heart attack, my girl, not a brain seizure!'

Natalie wasn't particularly reassured. She said, 'If—and I mean if—these extra horses come, where the hell are we going to put them?'

'In the new extension.'

'But that's only at the outline planning stage,' she protested.

'Not any more.' He poured himself some more coffee. 'I set the architect on preparing detailed drawings last week. Permission'll be a formality.'

'And financing?' she asked huskily. 'We're still paying off the accommodation block and...'

'And I've got a partner now. A partner with money.' He gave her a genial wink. 'This is going to be his pigeon, not mine, so stop panicking.'

The conversation had only served to bring home to Natalie with increasing emphasis how potent a force Eliot Lang was going to be at Wintersgarth.

Oh God, she thought savagely as she got into bed, why can't there be some sort of time slip? Why can't we go back to the time before Grantham had his heart attack, when everything was normal—and safe?

She switched off her light and settled herself for sleep, but it proved elusive. She found she was being tormented by vivid mental images of Eliot Lang locked together with his voluptuous blonde in some Harrogate hotel room.

When she did at last fall asleep, for the first time in many months she dreamed of Tony, and woke in the morning to find tears on her face.

The internal phone in the office rang and Natalie answered it, her mind still fixed on the farrier's bill in front of her. 'Yes, Beattie?'

'The removal van's arrived,' her stepmother announced triumphantly. 'Do you want to join me in a good pry?'

Natalie stifled a sigh. 'I—I haven't really got time.'

'Well, never mind.' Beattie sounded disappointed but cheerful. 'He's going to ask us to dinner when he's sorted himself out a bit, so we can see everything then.'

Hurrah, Natalie thought bleakly, as she replaced her receiver. The date on the calendar had been circled in red for quite some time now. There was no way she could forget that today was the day Eliot finally moved into Wintersgarth.

He'd been up several times in the intervening period, staying at the pub in the village. He had attended the planning hearing when permission for the stabling extension had been given, without problems as Grantham had predicted. He had checked on the progress of the decorators, and the firm he'd employed to install a new kitchen.

'I've seen the drawings,' Beattie had disclosed, awed. 'It looks more like the deck of a space ship than a kitchen!' She'd given the Aga an affectionate pat. 'I'd be afraid of pressing the wrong button!'

Natalie wasn't the world's greatest cook, and the culinary arrangements at the flat had been basic to say the least, but it still galled her that he was making such sweeping changes. But then everything he did seemed to find some raw spot, she thought ruefully, particularly as so far he hadn't seemed to put a foot wrong. She was ashamed to acknowledge that she'd harboured a secret hope that Wes and the lads would resent him, had looked forward to seeing him cut down to size in some subtle way. But it hadn't happened. He seemed to have hit the right note with them, as with everyone. Except herself.

She went back to the farrier's bill, but she couldn't concentrate. All she could think of was that the flying visits were over. Eliot was moving in, for good. And she would have to start thinking seriously about moving out.

She had dreaded having to face him again, after those few searing minutes in the tack room. She'd expected some pointed reminder, a look, a drawled remark. She'd been on edge waiting for it. But it hadn't happened— yet.

Perhaps Eliot had also had time to come to terms with a few things too. His attitude to her was polite, but briskly businesslike. He still, to her father's amusement, addressed her as Mrs Drummond.

'You're very formal, the pair of you,' he'd chided jovially. But it hadn't changed a thing. Natalie was as much a thorn in his flesh as he was in hers. But she wasn't driving him out of the only home he'd ever known, she thought bitterly.

At half past twelve, she closed the office and started up towards the house for lunch. The furniture van had gone, she saw, and Eliot's Porsche was parked outside the flat.

As she approached, a girl got out of the passenger seat and stood obviously waiting to speak to her. A mass of curling blonde hair hung to her shoulders, framing a full-lipped smiling face. She wore a ribbed wool dress, tightly cinched at the waist with a leather belt, thus drawing attention to well-shaped breasts and rounded hips. Her long legs were encased in high-heeled patent leather boots.

'Hello,' she said. 'I'm Sharon Endicott. Do you think you could show me where my things are to go? Eliot was going to, but he went up to the house to speak to Mr Slater, and he hasn't come back.'

Natalie swallowed. She said feebly, 'How do you do. I'm Natalie Drummond.'

The other girl nodded. 'I thought you would be.' She looked around. 'It's nice here.'

'Thank you,' Natalie managed feebly. She still couldn't assimilate that Eliot had actually brought his mistress with him. It seemed so—so blatant, somehow. And it would go down like a lead balloon with the locals, who were a pretty staid lot.

'Can you show me, then?' asked Sharon. 'I'd like to get unpacked, before everything creases.'

'Yes, of course. But wouldn't you prefer to wait for Mr—er—Lang?'

'It doesn't matter.' The girl shrugged shapely shoulders, grimacing slightly. 'He's probably forgotten all about me,' she confided without rancour. 'I wasn't supposed to be coming with him today, but I was free, so I thought I might as well, and save on the train fare later. I suppose I'm a bit of a surprise.'

You can say that again, Natalie muttered under her breath. Aloud she said, 'Have you just the one case? Then you go up here.'

Making no attempt to conceal her reluctance, she led the way up to the flat. It was like stepping into a different world from the one she remembered.

The big sitting-room was russet now, and the woodblock floor had been sanded and polished. There were no easy chairs as far as she could see, but two large sofas, deeply cushioned in cream hide. She noticed an antique writing desk, and a tall cabinet, beautifully inlaid, before she turned towards the bedroom.

The walls here were gold now, a warm shimmering colour that seemed to fill the room with sunlight, even though it was overcast outside. There was gold embroidery too on the predominantly cream quilted bedspread which had been flung over the wide bed. That, and the fact there were curtains hanging at the windows, revealed that Beattie hadn't been able to restrain her curiosity.

Natalie said, 'This is where you'll—sleep.' She despised herself for stumbling slightly over the word.

Sharon looked as if she'd been sandbagged as she gazed round her. She said slowly, 'Bloody hell.'

Perhaps their relationship had been confined to the impersonality of hotel rooms up to now, Natalie thought. Sharon was clearly shaken to see the kind of style Eliot enjoyed at home. She was rather taken aback herself.

She said, 'Well, make yourself at home. The kitchen's just down the hall.' She hesitated. 'I'm sorry you've been forgotten. If I see—Mr Lang, I'll jog his memory.'

'Oh, don't worry about it.' Sharon still sounded dazed. 'The horses come first with him, I know that.'

She didn't sound as if she minded either, Natalie thought, as she went back downstairs and emerged into the air. She stood for a moment drawing deep gulps of it into her lungs. She felt curiously at cross purposes with herself, and told herself it was seeing the home she had created with Tony so totally changed.

If Eliot was up at the house, she would go back to the office, she decided rather feverishly.

She turned the handle and walked in, stopping dead, as Eliot got up from the edge of her desk where he'd been sitting, and walked towards her.

'So there you are,' he observed. 'I thought perhaps you'd gone to lunch.'

'No.' Natalie lifted her chin. 'As a matter of fact, I've been seeing your—friend safely bestowed.'

'Oh.'' He looked faintly surprised. 'Well, that was good of you. Has she settled in all right?'

'I'd have thought that was your concern rather than mine,' Natalie said shortly. 'Why don't you go and see? The bed's made up and waiting for you.' She saw the dark brows snap together ominously, and clapped a hand over her mouth. 'Oh God, I'm sorry! Pretend I never said that. It's none of my business anyway what you do.'

'I'll second that,' he said coldly. 'Perhaps you'd be good enough to tell me what the hell you're talking about.'

'Sharon.' Natalie picked up a sheaf of papers and looked at them as if they were important. 'I—found her hanging round waiting for you, so I took her up to the flat. She—er—she goes very well with the décor,' she added desperately into an increasingly icy silence.

Eliot said, 'You took her up—to my *flat*? In God's name, why?' He closed his eyes for a moment. 'No, don't tell me. Let me guess. She's female, under fifty, no hump, no squint, therefore I must be having an affair with her. Is that how it reads?'

She felt herself beginning, hatefully, to blush, and turned away. 'As I said, it's really none of my business. This is the nineteen-eighties, after all...'

'Oh, but Sharon's very much your business,' he said, with a kind of awful calm. 'That's why I was looking for you—to give you these.' He handed her an envelope. He said savagely, 'Sharon's insurance card, Mrs Drummond. Her P45, and her references. Beddable though she undoubtedly is, I draw the line about sleeping with employees.' His voice lengthened into a sarcastic drawl. 'Sharon's a stable lad, Mrs Drummond, and a bloody good one. She was with a trainer I rode for regularly near Newbury. The horses she looked after there, however, are coming here next week, so I offered her the chance to come with them. I made her no other kind of offer, although heaven only knows what she's thinking now.' He took the envelope from Natalie's nerveless fingers and tossed it on to her desk. 'And now I suggest you get her out of my bedroom, offering whatever explanation seems good to you, and over to the blockhouse, where she belongs. And later, you and I will have a little talk.'

Natalie pressed her hands to her burning face. 'I'm sorry—I'm so *sorry*. It was just—she was there, and Andrew said you'd brought this blonde to Harrogate...' She broke off, staring at him imploringly.

'Then Andrew wants to be a damned sight more discreet,' said Eliot shortly. 'Now on you way, and let's see if you're as good at repairing damage as you are at causing it.'

In the end, it was easier than she could have hoped. Sharon good-naturedly accepted her stumbling excuses about 'a mistake' and was willingly shepherded to her rightful habitat.

'I knew it was too good to be true,' she said, as she put her case down on the narrow single bed with its colourful patchwork cover.

'I expect you're hungry.' Natalie prepared to make a hasty departure before Sharon asked any awkward questions about her original accommodation. 'There's plenty of stuff in the big freezer in the kitchen which you can just heat up in the microwave.'

'I'll find my way about. Don't worry about me,' Sharon assured her, as she unfastened her case and began to take out her things.

I'm not worried about you, thought Natalie as she made her way belatedly to the house for lunch. I'm wondering what Grantham is going to say when he hears he's had a girl lad foisted on him!'

But the expected eruption was not forthcoming.

'It's not what I like, or what I'm used to,' Grantham admitted when she tackled him. 'But these horses coming next week can be awkward beggars by all accounts, and Eliot tells me she handles them like an angel, so I'm prepared to give her a fair trial.'

A fair trial, Natalie thought wretchedly. A fair trial for her, but never for me.

Beattie said, 'I suggested to Eliot that he lunched with us today, but I think he wants to get the feel of his new home.' She smiled. 'I made his bed up for a welcome.' She gave Natalie a wicked wink. 'It's a very big bed— for a bachelor!'

Natalie was on the point of saying she'd seen it, but realised the admission would involve her in explanations she didn't feel equal to giving.

She said shortly, 'Perhaps he kicks like his damned horses,' and turned the conversation to the forthcoming Women's Institute handicrafts exhibition in which Beattie was heavily involved as a committee member.

But there was no way she could avoid the promised interview with Eliot later that afternoon. It was unpleasant but mercifully brief. She was told curtly to consult him before leaping to any more wild conclusions, and dismissed as if she'd been a naughty child.

So much for her resolution to avoid rocking the boat during her remaining time at Wintersgarth, Natalie thought, as she sank limply into her chair. Perhaps, this time, she had learned her lesson.

The two new horses arrived the following week, and were installed in their boxes by a frankly ecstatic Sharon. Their names were Thunderbird and Cupbearer, and they were the property, she told Natalie, of Oriel Prince.

'The actress?' Natalie was intrigued in spite of herself.

'There couldn't be two of her,' said Sharon with a certain amount of feeling. 'Old bitch. Well, she's not old,' she amended conscientiously. 'And she's in America just now, thank God, or she'd be up here like a rat up a drainpipe. Fancies Eliot something rotten, she does.' She giggled. 'They were supposed to have something going a while back. She used to come down while he was schooling the horses, and it was ''Darling this'' and ''Darling that'' and her hands all over him. Then she took up with some wealthy Arab.'

Natalie recalled in time that listening to gossip from Sharon was hardly a dignified occupation. She said, 'I don't care if she takes up with the entire United Arab Emirates as long as she pays her training bills,' and went back to the office.

Eliot's arrival in the locality had been enough of a sensation, she thought with a wry grin. If predatory actresses started descending too, the neighbours might never recover!

Already the invitations to cocktails and dinners had started to pour in, particularly from families with unmarried daughters, although she had to admit he was being selective about those he accepted.

'I can do without the social whirl,' he'd told Grantham, although he accepted, as her father did, that a certain amount of socialising was inevitable for the sake of public relations.

But if Natalie had expected him to spend every evening seeking out whatever entertainment was available locally, she was wrong. Apart from one foray to the village pub, where he'd played darts with the lads, he had seemed content to stay at home, getting the flat the way he wanted it, and playing music.

Beattie had been given the freedom of his hi-fi and record collection, and had come back starry-eyed. They had similar tastes, it appeared, and were already talking of joining forces to attend the forthcoming concert season in Leeds.

'Which will let you nicely off the hook, my darling,' said Beattie, dropping a kiss on her husband's head.

Natalie had hoped that Beattie's talk of a house-warming dinner at the flat had been imagination, but she was wrong.

'I'm going to have a rest tomorrow night,' her stepmother announced as she dished up the roast, with accompanying Yorkshire pudding, which invariably put Grantham into a good mood. 'We're dining with Eliot.'

'All of us?' Natalie took only one potato, feeling her appetite deserting her.

'Yes, of course,' said Beattie briskly. 'Why, did you have other plans?'

'Why, yes.' Natalie improvised swiftly. 'I thought I'd go into Harrogate to the cinema—the new Meryl Streep is on.'

'And will be for the rest of the week.' Grantham unfolded his napkin. 'If Eliot's making the effort to cook us a meal, lass, you can make the effort to eat it. It's time you two saw each other outside those office walls, anyway.' He encountered a look from his daughter and said hastily, 'Now I'm not asking you to marry him— just accept his hospitality, and be pleasant about it. That isn't too much to ask.'

Natalie cut up her food and pushed it round her plate in a pretence of eating. The office was safe, neutral territory. Meeting Eliot on his own ground, watching him play host in what had once been her home, was a frankly disturbing prospect. But one it seemed she could not avoid.

'Oh, are you wearing that dress?' said Beattie disappointedly when Natalie came downstairs the following evening.

Natalie glanced down at herself. 'What's wrong with it? It's a little basic black, the ideal thing for informal dinner parties—the saleswoman told me so herself.'

'Yes, but how many years ago?' Beattie asked gloomily. 'Darling, it's really time you went through your wardrobe, and treated yourself to some new things. You're so slim and your hair's gorgeous—you could wear some really exciting things.'

'If I had anything exciting to wear them for,' Natalie said drily. 'When I do, I'll consider it.'

She'd deliberately chosen the black dress because it was on the drab side. She wanted Eliot Lang to see that her evening self was just an extension of her subdued office persona. Then perhaps she'd be spared any future invitations.

All the same, she felt absurdly self-conscious as she followed Grantham and Beattie into the russet living-room. There was an autumnal nip in the air, and Eliot had kindled a log fire in the hearth. She loved the scent of woodsmoke. Tony had never cared for open fires, complaining they were messy, so they'd used a three-bar electric model instead.

She sank down on to one of the sofas, watching the leaping flames as Eliot served drinks.

'My own invention,' he told her, pouring out the contents of a cocktail shaker. 'I'm thinking of patenting it as the Wintersgarth Wallbanger.'

'Or fuel for Concorde,' said Beattie after a cautious sip. 'This is lethal, Eliot! What on earth is in it?'

'Let that be my little secret,' he said solemnly. He looked at Natalie. 'Care to take a chance, Mrs Drummond?'

'Now this is damned ridiculous,' Grantham said forcefully. 'We're out of office hours now, so let's drop all this "Mr and Mrs" nonsense. Her name's Natalie, lad, and you know it.'

'Yes, why not?' Eliot said slowly, his eyes fixed on her face. 'Shall we declare a truce?' He held out his hand, compelling her to respond. As his fingers closed round hers, Natalie found herself remembering with an odd inward shiver the last time he'd taken her hand—and seconds later, taken her mouth...

For a long moment, the hazel eyes looked enigmatically down into hers, holding her gaze as steadily as his hand clasped hers. Then, as if some unseen chain had been snapped, she was free, listening to Beattie asking him if the picture over the bureau was an original.

She'd wondered what kind of a cook he would turn out to be, and the tiny chickens, with their delectable fruit stuffing, and the wine-rich sauce soon gave her the answer. Even her father, who had been known to express opinions on 'fancy foreign muck', was reduced to appreciative grunts. And the blackberry mousse which preceded cheese and coffee was equally delicious.

'Congratulations.' Natalie added her contribution to the general plaudits. 'There seems to be no end to your talents.'

His oblique grin told her that he'd caught the faint acidity in her tone. He said quite gently, 'You don't know the half of them.'

I think, Natalie decided as she leaned back in her chair, away from the candlelit dinner table, to conceal her swift, involuntary blush, that I shall have 'I must not cross swords with Eliot Lang' tattooed across my forehead.

Beattie was gathering her resources. 'Now, Eliot dear, you must let me wash up for you. I insist.'

'There's no need,' he shook his head. 'All I have to do is load the dishwasher.'

'Then I'll do that,' she said briskly. 'Give me a hand to clear the table, Natalie, there's a love.'

Natalie hastened to comply. She would rather be flushed with activity, she thought, than because Eliot's sardonic gaze had told her quite explicitly that he could remember every detail of those moments in the tack room.

She was on her way back to the living-room foranother load when she noticed the bedroom door was open and light was pouring into the dim hallway. Feeling like a thief in the night, she paused at the door for another look. The bed was flanked now by two small but superbly made walnut chests of drawers, each carrying a silk-shaded lamp. The room seemed to glow—to beckon, she thought, her mouth going dry as she realised she was no longer alone. Eliot was standing beside her, when she'd thought he was safely in the living-room talking to her father.

She said nervously, 'I'm sorry, you must think I'm unforgivably nosy...'

He cut across her stumbling words. He said harshly, 'Was it like this—the room—when you slept here with Tony Drummond? Was the furniture in the same place?'

The question was an outrage, she thought. He had no right, no right in the world to ask her about such an intimate subject. Her lips parted to tell him so.

She heard herself say, 'No, it was quite different. The—the bed was on the other wall, beneath the window.'

Eliot nodded abruptly, his eyes never leaving her face. He said, 'That's good. I want it to be different. I don't want even the slightest comparison to be drawn—when you come here to me.'

His hand touched her face in a caress so fleeting, Natalie thought afterwards that she'd imagined it.

Then he turned and left her, stunned and speechless, staring after him.

CHAPTER FOUR

NATALIE lingered over breakfast the next morning, and found herself inventing excuses for not going immediately down to the stable office as she normally did.

The rest of the previous evening had passed off without incident. In fact, Natalie kept asking herself if that moment in the passage hadn't been some bizarre hallucination. When she eventually returned to the living-room with Beattie, she found Eliot had reverted to being no more than the courteous host to them all.

He'd been wasted in National Hunt racing, Natalie told herself furiously. He should have been an actor—or a chameleon. Fortunately Grantham and Beattie were enjoying themselves so much that they didn't notice her protracted silence, or at any rate didn't question it. But she was thankful when they reluctantly took their leave, just before eleven.

Now she glanced at her watch, and decided she really couldn't delay any longer. With any luck Eliot would already have ridden out to exercise.

But luck wasn't running her way. The string was only just making its way out of the yard, and up towards the moor. As Natalie passed, Sharon led Thunderbird out of his box. Her usually sunny smile of greeting was subdued.

Natalie paused. 'Is something wrong?' She glanced at Thunderbird. He was stepping well, and he gleamed with health. 'He's all right, isn't he?'

'He's thriving. He seems to love it here.' Sharon hesitated. 'But I think I'm going to have to leave.'

'Oh!' Natalie's heart sank. Sharon's employment at Wintersgarth had represented the first chink in Grantham's chauvinist armour. 'I—I suppose it is rather quiet here. Are you lonely?'

'Oh, no.' Sharon shook her head vigorously. 'Everyone's really friendly, and Wes's wife Chris has gone out of her way to make me feel at home.'

'Then what is it?' Natalie persisted.

Sharon glanced round, but no one else was within earshot. She said, 'It sounds really stupid, but in the blockhouse, there's a Peeping Tom—at least I think there is.'

'Oh.' Natalie digested this for a moment. 'What makes you think so?'

Sharon sighed. 'I was in the bath two nights ago. I locked the bathroom door as I always do, but I caught the edge of the towel on the key, and it fell out of the lock. I just left it, because I was in a bit of a hurry.' She paused. 'I was just washing my hair when I had the weirdest feeling that someone was looking through the keyhole at me.'

Natalie bit her lip. 'Did you hear any voices—sniggering?'

'No.' Sharon shook her head. 'I could have coped with that—asked them if they'd seen enough, told them to grow up—but it wasn't like that. It was just—silence.'

'What did you do?'

'I just stayed where I was,' Sharon admitted ruefully. 'There was plenty of lather, what with the shampoo and that. Then eventually I felt that whoever it was had gone.' She shivered. 'The water was cold by then, though.'

'Well, I can only apologise,' said Natalie. 'But please don't do anything hasty. Maybe it was just an isolated incident and...'

'But it isn't,' Sharon interrupted unhappily. 'Last night someone tried to get into my room. I thought I'd have an early night—write a couple of letters home, and I just had the little bedside lamp on. Well, I must have dozed off, but I woke up about midnight. I turned over to switch the lamp off, and I saw the door handle turning, ever so slowly, and the whole door moved just a bit as if somebody had pushed against it, testing whether it was locked.'

'Which it was.'

'Oh, yes, I always turn the key when I'm on my own. At my last place, I shared with two other girls, and I'm in with my sister at home.'

'How long did it go on for?'

'Quite a while.' Sharon paused. 'Well, it seemed like it, but I dare say it was only a minute or two really. Whoever it was just kept twisting the handle backwards and forwards. And this time I did speak. I said "Who's that?" ever so loudly, and I heard someone run away.' She shook her head, her candid eyes fixed on Natalie's face. 'But it gave me a turn, and I didn't like it.'

'I wouldn't have liked it either,' Natalie admitted, with a grimace. She thought for a moment. 'Have you any idea who it could be? Have any of the lads...'

'Come sniffing round?' Sharon supplied. 'Not really. I'm older than a few of them, and I made it clear at the start, without being nasty, that I was here to work, and I wasn't interested in anything else.'

'Obviously someone interpreted that as encouragement,' Natalie said with a sigh. 'If we can get this sorted out, would you be prepared to stay then?'

Sharon looked doubtful. 'I don't see how it can be sorted, without causing an awful atmosphere, and I wouldn't want to do that. Besides, even if I did find out who it was, he'd probably say he meant it as a joke. But I don't want to leave, and that's the truth.'

'Then leave it with me—please.' Natalie patted her arm. 'And now you'd better get off, or Wes will be shouting at the pair of us.'

'At last!' Eliot snapped impatiently, as she entered the office. He was sitting on the edge of her desk, one booted leg swinging, fingers drumming briskly. 'I began to think you'd decided not to work today.'

'I almost did,' she said shortly. 'Is it something urgent?'

'Rather more essential than your gossip with Sharon,' he said brusquely. 'I'd like you to call the vet, and ask him to look at Murgatroyd's Lad. He cast in his box last night, and is going lame. I don't think it's too serious, but I want to make sure. And would you also give the builders a blast for me. I want a start made on those new loose boxes.'

'Yes, sir. Right away, sir.' Natalie sketched a salute. 'And I was not gossiping,' she added hotly. 'Sharon had a problem she wanted to talk over.'

'Then she should bring them to Grantham or myself,' he returned. 'We pay her wages. Besides, you have problems enough of your own. What was so important as to keep Thunderbird hanging round in the yard for nearly ten minutes?'

'I can handle it.'

'Your faith in your abilities is so touching, sweetheart. Is she unhappy? Is it the lack of night life?'

Although she was still smarting from his jibe, Natalie felt her lips twitch involuntarily. 'Far from it,' she said drily. 'Someone's been spying on her. Peering through the bathroom keyhole—trying her door at night—that kind of thing.' She paused. 'Sexual harassment is the jargon phrase, I believe.'

Eliot said something rude and succinct under his breath. 'Well, that can stop before it begins,' he said angrily. 'Does she have the least idea who it is?'

Natalie shook her head.

'Do you?' The question was sharp enough to make her jump slightly.

'Er—no.' But it wasn't altogether true. She herself had been made to feel uneasy, more than once.

'That could have been spoken with more conviction.' Eliot gave her a long look. 'Is Sharon very upset?'

'Upset enough to be talking about going back down South.'

His lips tightened. 'That's not going to happen. She's too damned valuable to be driven away by some adolescent with his brains in his pants.' He walked to the door, then swung back towards Natalie. 'But you won't deal with this. I will.'

'Do you think you're quite the right person to take this high moral stance?' Natalie asked coolly.

His brows lifted. 'Snooping round keyholes has never been my style, darling. If I want to look at a girl taking a bath, I make sure the tub's big enough for two.'

Natalie's cheeks warmed faintly. She looked down at the pile of unopened envelopes in front of her. 'I didn't mean that. I meant—you're quite adept at sexual harassment yourself.'

'In what way?' He leaned against the door jamb as if he had all the time in the world.

'You know quite well,' she protested. 'Last night you made an unpleasant—an unforgivable remark.'

'Ah,' he smiled. 'But that wasn't harassment, sweetheart. That was a prophecy.'

She tore open one of the envelopes, ripping its contents in her haste.

'Kindly understand this,' she said, her voice shaking. 'Under no circumstances will I sleep with you—ever!'

His smile widened. 'Who mentioned sleeping?' he murmured, and went out, slamming the door behind him.

Natalie seethed, she simmered, she was incandescent with rage.

Why do I do it? she wailed inwardly. Why do I set myself up?

Well, it would not happen again, she promised herself. After all, it was damaging to allow herself to be upset over what was only a little cheap teasing. Because Eliot had no serious intentions towards her. Curvy blondes were his type of woman, not skinny redheads. It was just the type of man who couldn't resist verbal advances to anything in a skirt, and she despised him for it. She despised all men who needed women not as people but as a boost to their macho egos.

She glanced down and saw that the pencil she'd been holding had snapped in two in her taut fingers.

She took a deep breath, and tossed the pieces into the waste basket. She could not afford to let him get to her like that again. From now on she would be deaf to the promise in the cool, drawling voice, the amused invitation in the hazel eyes. And eventually, when he was faced by a wall of blank indifference, Eliot would, she hoped, transfer his advances to some more willing lady.

Or should she try shock tactics, with the truth? Look him straight in the eye, and say, 'It's no use trying to seduce me, because I'm immune. I know the kisses and the sweet talk for what they are—the big build-up to the big let-down. All during my marriage I tried to enjoy sex and failed completely. I used to dread going to bed at night. I used to pray that he'd leave me alone—not touch me. Our whole relationship was a sham, and as a wife, I was the biggest phoney of all. In fact, my husband's last words to me before he stormed out of the house that day were, "It's your own fault, you frigid little bitch!"'

The old nausea, the old trembling began all over again, and she pressed her hand convulsively over her mouth. Eliot Lang had succeeded in reviving memories she'd hoped were buried for ever. Memories that should have been buried.

Memories that would be...

She telephoned the vet, who said he would call early that afternoon. She called the builder, who said work on the new looseboxes would be started the following day. She dealt with the mail, moving like an automaton.

It would be healthier, she thought, to concentrate on her other grievances where Eliot was concerned. The way he'd dismissed her involvement with Sharon's problem, for instance, still rankled.

He might be the boss, but he was still a comparative stranger to the yard. His relationship with the stable lads was predominantly a working one. Most of them had been at Wintersgarth for some time, so it was natural she should know more about their lives and personalities than he did. She knew which of them were courting local girls, and which of them preferred to spend their free time adventuring in Leeds. And she also had her feminine instinct to go on.

I'd bet a month's salary I know who it is who's pestering Sharon, she thought as Ben Watson's image presented itself. It wasn't just the way he looked at her. There was a television and video set in the recreation room at the blockhouse, and she'd heard whispers of late-night blue movie sessions, with films Ben had brought back from his day off. And not that long ago she had found two of the youngest lads goggling over girlie magazines of the most lurid and explicit kind. When she'd questioned them rather sharply, they had admitted Ben had lent them to them. These were things Eliot had no means of knowing.

And it was herself that Sharon had turned to, after all, so help her she would.

She rested her elbows on her desk and rested her chin on her clasped hands, as she pondered what to do. It would be useless to accuse Ben directly. Sharon had seen no one, and there was no actual proof, so all he would need to do would be to protest his injured innocence.

Although a confrontation might warn him off from any future prying, she thought dubiously. But he would still be around, a sly and distasteful influence, especially on the younger and more impressionable lads.

And she couldn't simply request Grantham to fire him, as there was nothing wrong with his work. His horses were well turned out, and Wes, who was a stickler for standards, had no real complaints about him, because she'd checked during Grantham's absence.

But if he could be caught in the act, she could insist that he was dismissed. The trick, of course, was catching him. She thought for a while longer, then nodded. She would see Sharon later during the rest period before evening stables and tell her what she had in mind.

And all Sharon had to do was agree.

'I feel a real fool,' said Sharon, three nights later. 'Maybe I imagined the whole thing. There's no need for you to bother any more, Miss Natalie. Why don't you give up, and go back up to the house?'

Natalie smiled as she put her flashlight down on the bedside table. 'Because I refuse to be defeated so easily,' she returned. 'I'll give it one more night, and if there's nothing we'll assume that Mr X has given up in disgust.'

Sharon lingered, frowning. 'But I know Eliot wouldn't like it if he knew,' she said abruptly. 'He was talking to me about it only today—asking if there'd been any trouble, and telling me I was to go straight to him, if so. I didn't know where to put my face.'

'Oh, he won't mind,' Natalie said mendaciously, 'Now, off you go, and get a good night's sleep.'

After another doubtful look, Sharon departed to take up temporary quarters in one of the unoccupied rooms, as she'd done for the last two nights.

It was all a bit like Fourth Form pranks in the dorm, Natalie thought with self-mockery, as she stretched out on top of Sharon's bed. Going up to her room at the house on the pretext of having an early night, then creeping out later without being seen, and making her way down to the blockhouse. Only there was no mid-night feast to look forward to, only hours of uneasy dozing as she waited vainly for the unlocked door to open. And when it did, and the flashlight had revealed who the unknown molester was, she had rehearsed a short but pithy speech, culminating in an order to present himself at the office in the morning for his cards.

She sighed, as she moved into a more comfortable position. At least her scheme had given her a chance to test the lads' accommodation at first hand. Didn't they say you should always sleep in your own spare bed before offering it to a guest? she thought, grinning to herself. Well, there was nothing the matter with this bed, even if it was narrower than she was accustomed to.

She hadn't much in the way of camouflage clothes, so she'd put on a black velvet lounging suit which she'd bought on impulse, and never worn, and she'd tied her hair up in a black silk scarf. She removed this now, shaking the copper waves over her shoulders, and turned on to her side, watching the door. In her heart she was beginning to agree with Sharon that she was probably wasting her time. Ben, if it was Ben, would have taken fright when Sharon called out, realising that she was a girl with a healthy pair of lungs who could scream the block down if her assailant had got into her room. And he knew she kept her door locked, so he'd be a fool to try again, and she was an even bigger idiot for thinking so.

She heard the others come up to bed, heard the jokes, the small scuffles and 'goodnights' before everything went quiet for the night.

And eventually, Natalie's eyelids drooped, and she too slept.

To be woken by a hand, stiflingly over her mouth. Her eyes flew open, her body rigid with panic, as she registered the voice whispering gloatingly in her ear.

'You want it, don't you? That's why you left your door open, because you knew I'd be back. You want this.' His other hand groped obscenely under the velvet top, and Natalie's body jack-knifed in sheer revulsion. She bit violently at the smothering hand, at the same time making a grab for the flashlight.

He swore disgustingly, and hit her across the face so hard her head sang. But the flashlight was in her hand, and desperately she clicked on the switch, sending a beam of light straight into Ben Watson's startled eyes. He blinked, flinching away, and it gave her the chance to push away the clammily exploring hand and roll across the bed. She stood up, keeping the light trained on him.

She'd forgotten everything she intended to say. His touch seemed to be all over her. She felt polluted. Her voice cracking, she said, 'Be at the office tomorrow, Watson. You're leaving. And don't ask for a reference.'

For a moment he stiffened, then he switched on the bedside lamp and stood staring at her.

'Well, well,' he said softly. 'If it isn't Miss Toffee-nosed Natalie herself! Miss Iced Diamond.'

'Never mind that,' she said sharply. 'Get out of here, and be glad I don't have you charged with attempted rape.'

'Rape?' There was something more than a sneer in his voice. 'It wouldn't be rape, you bitch, and you know it. You ask for it, all of you, walking round, flaunting yourselves, thinking yourselves so bloody high and mighty.' His voice thickened. 'What's the matter? Were you jealous Sharon might be getting something you weren't? Well, you only had to tip me the wink. I've always fancied you, but you knew that, didn't you—treating me like I was dirt.'

'You are dirt.' Natalie kept her voice steady with an effort. 'Now get back to your own quarters.'

'All in good time.' He was far too much at ease, she thought with sudden fear. 'We're on our own. You can drop the play-acting. I know what you need. It's been a long time, hasn't it, since that husband of yours picked the wrong time to use that unmanned crossing? You've been missing it. And now, here you are.' He giggled, and the hair rose on the nape of her neck. 'It's like backing a bloody outsider and winning the tote jackpot.' He started to move towards her. 'So let's forget about me leaving, shall we? By tomorrow you might not want me to.'

Natalie lifted her chin. 'Keep away from me, Watson!'

'Try and make me—Drummond.' His tone was vicious. 'You've robbed me of my bit of fun, so the least you can do is make it up to me.'

She'd never noticed before how stocky he was, how broad-shouldered. She took a firmer grip on the heavy flashlight. She wanted to scream, but the muscles of her throat didn't seem to be working properly. She'd heard panic could do that to you, but she'd never believed it until that moment, with Ben Watson closing on her, grinning, running his tongue round his lips.

As he reached her, she swung the flashlight at him, but he grabbed her wrist, twisting it cruelly, making her gasp with pain. She kicked at him, but the light-soled shoes she was wearing made little impression. Her struggles just seemed to amuse him.

He threaded his hand through her hair, pulling her head painfully backwards, and she felt his mouth, hot and wet, on her exposed throat. And this time she did scream, a strangled thread of sound.

Then the door erupted open, and the room seemed suddenly full of people. She saw Eliot's dark, furious face, then Ben Watson was tumbling backwards, lying on the rug, with a trickle of blood coming from the corner of his mouth.

Eliot caught Natalie by the shoulders. 'Are you all right?' His voice was hoarse, totally unlike his own. She nodded weakly, tried to say something and failed.

'Take her,' he said to Sharon, who had stayed near the door, looking hangdog. 'Sit her on the bed and put her head between her knees for a moment or two while I deal with this scum.'

Natalie saw him reach down, jerking Watson to his feet by the front of his shirt, and closed her eyes, feeling sick.

'Don't,' she managed to croak. 'Oh God, don't! Just get him out of here. Get rid of him.'

The hazel eyes were blazing. 'I'm calling the police.'

'No, you can't. We have to think of Grantham. I—I won't press charges. Just make sure I don't have to see him again.'

There was a loaded silence, then Eliot turned to Sharon. 'When Miss Natalie can walk, take her back to the house. Mrs Slater will look after her.'

'She'll be in bed.' Natalie found she wanted to burst into tears. 'We mustn't wake her.'

'Don't be a damned fool,' he said crushingly. 'How do you think I knew you were missing?' He gave Natalie one last furious look, then left the room, propelling Ben Watson in front of him.

'He isn't half mad,' Sharon said gloomily. 'I'm going to be in dead lumber tomorrow.'

'It is tomorrow.' Natalie hauled herself wearily to her feet. 'It's all right, Sharon. I'll tell him I talked you into it, that you had no choice.'

Sharon didn't look wholly comforted. She said, 'I thought I heard something, so I'd come out into the corridor to see, when he came up those stairs like a crazy man. He said, "She's here, isn't she? Don't bother to lie."' She shivered. 'I thought he was going to kill me!'

I know he's going to kill me, Natalie thought despondently as she made her way back to the house, where Beattie was waiting anxiously, the drawing-room fire ready re-kindled. She listened in appalled silence to Natalie's stumbling story, then went and fetched her a glass of brandy. She also had one herself.

'I need it,' she said grimly. 'Nat darling, didn't you realise the risks you could be running? You could have been raped!'

Natalie shuddered. 'Yes, I know that now. But up till now, I'd always looked on Ben Watson as someone—vaguely unpleasant—the sort of little weasel who'd get his kicks through playing at Peeping Tom. It never occurred to me he could be—dangerous.'

'Thank God Eliot turned up when he did.'

'I—suppose so.' Natalie looked down at her glass. She said, 'Why did you contact him?'

Beattie looked thoroughly embarrassed. 'Mother hen instinct,' she said reluctantly. 'I went to your room to see if you had any paracetamol. I seemed to be starting a headache, and I'd run out. I felt it was odd your bed hadn't been slept in, when you'd made such a thing about having an early night.' She flushed. 'I could see the lights were on in Eliot's flat—and I thought that was where you were,' she went on in a little rush, avoiding Natalie's gaze. 'I don't know what made me phone him to check. I felt an awful busybody. After all, you're a grown woman with your own life to lead, but I just felt so uneasy—because it wasn't *like* you.' She paused. 'And I'm so thankful I did phone. Eliot seemed to know at once where you'd be.'

Natalie bit her lip. 'You thought I'd got some sordid little assignation going? Beattie, how could you?'

Beattie looked bewildered. 'But it wouldn't have been so extraordinary,' she insisted. 'I thought the two of you seemed to be getting on much better together at the dinner party. And he is incredibly attractive, Nat. I wouldn't have blamed you at all, although Grantham

might have,' she added with a little grimace. 'The poor
darling thinks he's still living in the Victorian age where
his womenfolk are concerned.'

'Then he doesn't have to worry,' Natalie said briefly.
'My own ideas are pretty antediluvian too.' She swallowed. 'I find it amazing that you can be so horrified
at the idea of Ben Watson—mauling me, yet accept that
Eliot Lang could have been—degrading me in exactly
the same way.'

Beattie sat bolt upright. 'Nat!' Her voice shook. 'It
isn't the same thing at all, darling.'

'Isn't it? It seems so from my viewpoint. One fate is
no worse than the other.'

Beattie put her glass down very slowly, as she considered her reply. 'You're still upset, darling,' she said,
'or I'm sure you wouldn't be saying these things. You've
been married. You know that there's a vast gulf between
making love with a man in a state of mutual desire, and
being—used for the gratification of some selfish, violent
lust.'

Natalie said quietly, 'Is there? I'll have to take your
word for it.' She put down her glass and rose to her feet.
'Thanks for the brandy, Beattie. Perhaps it will help me
to sleep.'

If anything could, she thought as she went upstairs,
with the prospect of Eliot's anger to face in a few hours'
time.

CHAPTER FIVE

NATALIE'S eyes felt as if they'd been rubbed with sand-paper, and her head ached as she went into the office. The door to the inner room stood ajar, and Grantham's voice raised and angry came booming through.

'I always said no good would come of employing lasses, and I was damned right! It's just putting temptation in the way, and it's cost me a good lad. Well, the girl can go too. I'm not having any more of this kind of bother!'

She heard Eliot say quietly, 'No.'

'I'm glad you agree with me.'

'I don't. I was responding to your suggestion that Sharon should be dismissed.'

There was a pause. The lull before the storm, Natalie thought, bracing herself.

'What the hell do you mean?' roared Grantham.

'Exactly what I say. Sharon stays.'

'And who the hell are you to tell me what to do in my own stables? I'll have no lax discipline here!'

'I'm your partner,' Eliot returned coolly, 'not some underling to jump to attention whenever you raise your voice. And I'm satisfied that Sharon did nothing to lead Watson on. Therefore I don't intend to allow her to be penalised. And that's my final word on the subject.'

'Is it? Is it, by God? Then let me tell you...' Grantham's voice was rising to ominous levels.

Natalie pushed the door wide and walked into the room. Grantham, red with anger, turned on her. 'And what do you want?'

Natalie lifted her chin and looked him straight in the eye. She said, 'If Sharon goes, I go. Ben Watson didn't confine his attentions to her alone, Dad. And I can promise you, I certainly didn't encourage him, and I'm sure Sharon didn't either.' She touched the tip of her tongue to dry lips. 'Eliot is quite right.'

Eliot glanced down at the riding whip he was holding, his face expressionless.

Grantham sat down heavily in his chair. She saw with relief the worst of the florid colour begin to fade from his face.

'Are you telling me that—scum dared to make advances to my daughter?' He struck the desk with his clenched fist, jarring a silver tankard stuffed with pens. 'If I could get my hands on him . . .'

Natalie glanced at Eliot in alarm, and was reassured by his faint shake of the head. Ben Watson, it was clear, had already left Wintersgarth.

She said steadily, 'Sharon may not be your daughter, but she's an employee, as I am, and entitled to the same kind of respect and protection. If it's not forthcoming, there's no point in my remaining here either.'

Grantham glared at her. 'Don't you dictate to me, my girl!'

'I wouldn't dream of it. But Beattie will—if I tell her that you've been getting worked up and shouting your head off, in spite of all the promises you made the consultant.' She put a teasing note in her voice, but Grantham was not mollified.

He said heavily, 'I never thought I'd see the day when I'd be crossed by a lad half my age.' He gave Natalie a look. 'And blackmailed by my own flesh and blood.' He pointed at the papers on his desk. 'I came down to do the entries for Wetherby, but you might as well take over—as you seem to be doing with everything else!' He got up and strode out of the room, slamming the door behind him. The heard the outer door bang shut too.

Eliot said drily, 'The honeymoon would appear to be over.'

Natalie said defensively, 'You can't blame him. He's always been in charge—always number one. He's never deferred to anyone, not even the owners. It's hard for him. You have to make allowances.'

'I thought I had been doing,' said Eliot. 'Otherwise this little blow-up would have come much sooner, believe me. If Grantham wanted a yes-man, a subordinate rather than a partner, he should have approached someone else.' He paused. 'But thank you for your unexpected support.'

Natalie looked down at the floor. 'It seemed the least I could do—after last night.' She swallowed. 'I—I was very relieved to see you.' Her voice became husky. 'And I'm sorry that Beattie—jumped to conclusions about where I was. It won't happen again.'

'How true,' he said sardonically. 'I'm sure you couldn't wait to disabuse her mind of that particular notion.' He paused. 'Tell me, did you know that Watson was going to be your uninvited guest?'

'I didn't know,' she said. 'I couldn't be sure. But I had this feeling about him that I couldn't explain—a prejudice, really.'

Eliot flicked his riding whip gently against his gleaming boot. 'It didn't occur to you to—share this feeling with anyone?'

'It didn't seem fair when I had no proof,' Natalie said defensively. 'And naturally, I didn't want to agitate my father unnecessarily.' She stopped suddenly. 'Oh!'

'Precisely,' he said levelly. 'I've just had to remind Grantham, and now it's your turn. Whether you wish it or not, Natalie, I'm here, and I intend to remain here. The sooner you come to terms with that fact, the better it will be for all of us.' The hazel eyes looked at her coldly. 'Life is complicated enough without having to cope with your resentment, silent and verbal, day in, day out. I thought I'd warned you off involving yourself any further in this Peeping Tom business, but I should have known that after one word from me, you'd do as you liked. You could have consulted me over your intuition about Watson, but that never occurred to you, did it?'

Natalie's cheeks burned. She stared down at the strip of carpet. 'No.'

Eliot said very wearily, 'Exactly. If your stepmother hadn't chanced to go into your room, you could have been very seriously assaulted. You could have been raped. And you can imagine the effect that would have had on Grantham's heart condition.'

She bit her lip. 'You don't have to say all this. Beattie's already...'

'Beattie couldn't be hard on you if she tried,' he said brusquely. 'And that's what you need. Just be thankful I'm confining myself to words alone. What I'm tempted to do is give you the bloody good hiding you so richly deserve.'

'How dare you!' she said hoarsely.

'Quite easily, sweetheart, believe me.' The whip flicked again. 'You're headstrong, Natalie. You like to take the bit between your teeth and run, and last night you nearly charged into disaster. And if it was just down to me, I'd probably let you,' he added dispassionately. 'But for your father's sake, and Beattie's, I can't allow it. So regard this as your final warning, lady. Do the work you're paid for, and don't meddle in what doesn't concern you.'

'So I'm just the office girl,' she said unevenly.

'For the present,' he agreed. 'Until you can prove your judgement can be trusted.'

She flung her head up. 'And who says I have to trust you? The builders may have started on the new extension, but where are the horses which are going to fill it? We haven't been exactly stampeded by new owners since you joined us.'

'Nor do we want to be,' he said calmly. 'Until the new boxes are built, anyway. But you don't have to worry, Natalie. The horses will come. Now, I'd better get on with those entries. If you could rustle up some coffee, I'd be grateful.'

He didn't look up again, and after a moment she turned and left the room.

She found she was breathing far too quickly, and her forehead and the palms of her hands felt damp and clammy. She leaned for a second against the bulk of the filing cabinet, trying to regain her equilibrium. If he'd shouted and sworn at her, she could have understood it better. She was used, after all, to weathering Grantham's storms. But Eliot's cool, almost laconic approach left her bewildered, and oddly crushed.

She'd behaved like a complete fool, and he'd let her know it. And the only crumb of comfort she could derive from the whole wretched episode was that it seemed, at last, to have killed off any transient desire he might have felt for her stone dead.

But somehow, even that was no longer the reassurance it would once have been, she thought with a little shaken sigh. And, on that discomfiting reflection, went to put the kettle on.

Grantham seemed subdued in the weeks that followed. There were no more confrontations between Eliot and himself, however, to Natalie's relief. And Eliot's attitude towards herself had been as coolly professional and businesslike as she could have wished.

But the last thing she expected was for Grantham to announce out of a blue sky that he and Beattie were going away the following weekend to visit Beattie's sister in Worcestershire.

'She's been asking us to go for long enough,' he muttered. 'And it's unfair to Beattie to keep turning her invitations down.'

Natalie stared at him. 'But there's racing at Lassiter Park next Saturday. We have three entries.'

'Well, Eliot can manage.' Grantham didn't meet her eye. 'After all, what's the point of having a younger man as a partner if I can't relax—take things a bit easier sometimes, tell me that?'

Natalie wasn't prepared to tell him anything at all. For the first time, it occurred to her that Grantham might seriously be considering a kind of semi-retirement. Up to then, she had believed that her father would hang on tooth and nail, fighting every inch of the way to retain control over what he still regarded as his.

This new departure, she thought, stemmed from the disagreement over Sharon, and for a moment she felt a flicker of guilt, wondering if her intervention that morning had influenced his decision.

But if he was genuinely easing up, it could only be for his ultimate benefit, she told herself decisively. Nor was there any way he would retire altogether while there was breath in his body.

'And I've told Eliot you'll go to Lassiter Park with him,' Grantham added too casually.

'You did what?' Natalie shook her head in disbelief.

'What's the problem?' her father rumbled. 'You used to have enough to say when I didn't let you go. Made me think I'd blighted your life.'

She said, 'That was—different.'

'I'm damned if I see how,' he said. 'Well, you can go, and do the social thing with the owners and their wives. They like that, and Eliot will have his hands full with the horses.'

Natalie began to protest, met his fulminating gaze, and subsided. There was no point in arguing, she thought, and if it was any consolation, Eliot would be no more pleased to have her foisted on him than she was. And it was only one day they had to spend together. Eliot rarely came up to the house except for the odd meal or cup of coffee, and she certainly wouldn't be cooking for him during Beattie's absence.

Eliot came into the office while she was engrossed in the wages ledger, and stood looking down at her.

'I hear I'm to have the pleasure of your company at the races,' he remarked expressionlessly.

Natalie said defensively, 'It wasn't my idea.'

'I never imagined it would be.' He gave her a searching look. 'On the other hand, a day in the fresh air might do you good. You don't seem to go out much.'

She put her pen down. 'Please don't feel sorry for me. I'm not a charity case.'

His mouth tightened. 'Nothing was further from my thoughts,' he assured her shortly. 'And I'm sure you can think of a last-minute excuse to remain here, if you really put your mind to it.'

As he turned away, she said huskily, 'I'm sorry. I—I'd really like to go. It's been ages since I saw any racing, except on television.'

He looked down at her. 'Then we'll consider it an arrangement,' he said quietly. 'There isn't always an ulterior motive in everything I say to you. You've been looking rather pale in recent days, that's all. You don't always need to keep your nose quite so firmly fixed to the grindstone. You make me feel like a slavedriver.'

She said, 'It's probably that whip you carry all the time.'

For a moment he looked astounded, then he burst out laughing and placed the offending item ceremoniously on her desk. 'I shall have to watch that,' he said, and disappeared.

Natalie found she was smiling over the PAYE several minutes later, and rebuked herself hastily.

Just because he chose to exert his charm where she was concerned, it didn't change a thing, she reminded herself defensively. And it was oddly disturbing that he'd noticed she was looking peaky, when she'd been convinced he'd barely spared her a second glance lately.

She opened her desk drawer, took out a small pocket mirror, and studied herself for a moment. The fact that she hadn't slept well since Ben Watson's departure had taken its toll of her, she had to admit. There were shadows under her eyes, and her cheekbones looked more prominent than ever.

She sighed. Perhaps she would see the doctor, get some of the sleeping tablets he'd prescribed after Tony's accident. And a tonic too, maybe. And she quelled the unbidden thought that a day at Lassiter Park with Eliot might be just what she needed.

The following Saturday was a mild day, with a misty sun gleaming through the bare branches of the trees. Lassiter Park wasn't a big course, but its facilities were excellent, and a big crowd had been attracted to watch the racing.

Grantham had driven off the day before, not without a last-minute struggle. 'It'll be the first meeting I've missed since I broke my shoulder,' he'd declared belligerently, then glared at Eliot as if it was somehow his fault. 'You've got that list of instructions?'

Eliot nodded impassively. It had, Natalie reflected, with a smothered grin, been read over to him so many times, he probably knew it by heart.

'And tell Clark Johnson to give La Margarita an easy race over the first half, or she'll run herself out of steam!' Grantham bellowed from the car window as Beattie drove him firmly away.

Now, in the parade ring, Eliot was presumably doing just that, she thought, watching him chat to Clark Johnson, a baby-faced rider just out of his apprenticeship. And if Clark did what he was told, La Margarita could provide Wintersgarth with its first win of the afternoon. She hoped it would happen. The owner was there with his wife and teenage sons, all bubbling over with excitement.

Eliot himself looked very relaxed, but he must be suffering a certain amount of tension, Natalie thought. He'd been very quiet on the drive down to the course, closed up in his own thoughts. Or maybe he just didn't like to chat while he was driving. Natalie had been well content to sit and admire the October countryside rather than maintain her half of a potentially awkward conversation.

Once they arrived at Lassiter Park, she had half expected to be left to her own devices, but instead Eliot had escorted her to the saddling boxes, so that they could both see how the horses had settled after their journey. Now, half-way through the afternoon, she had to admit he'd done his best to make her feel she was part of the team, instead of an unwanted encumbrance.

Although he would undoubtedly have had a much better time if she'd not been so constantly at his side, she thought acidly. It had almost seemed at one point as if every woman at the meeting had made some excuse to come and speak to him, a number of them with distinctly predatory gleams in their eyes. And she had to concede an unwilling admiration for the way Eliot had dealt with all this attention. He had been polite and sufficiently charming not to dash any lady's hopes, but that was as far as it had gone. And he'd made a point of introducing Natalie to each and every one of them, without, she'd realised, mentioning the fact that she was his partner's daughter.

'Am I your chaperon?' she had asked after a while, struggling with her amusement.

'Perish the thought,' Eliot returned, slanting a wicked grin at her.

'Well, if they decide to award a prize for the most hated female under forty, I know who'll get it,' she said wryly.

Eliot turned and looked at her, a slow comprehensive stare which took in all of her, from the swirl of copper hair piled up on her head to the toes of her chestnut-coloured boots, including the brand new and very expensive suit she'd treated herself to in moss green, velvet-soft suede, with its straight skirt and gently bloused jacket.

He said quietly, 'It isn't the only prize you'd win today.'

She felt swift, embarrassed colour flare in her cheeks, and hurriedly transferred her attention to her race card, hoping desperately that Eliot wouldn't think she'd been fishing for some kind of compliment.

Because she hadn't dressed for him, she thought confusedly, but for the credit of Wintersgarth as a whole.

Now, as he came back to her side, she looked up, forcing a smile.

'Shall we go back to the stand?' He put a hand under her elbow, guiding her through the throng of people. As he did so, they came face to face with a tall, pretty girl in a fur coat. As she saw them, all the colour seemed to drain out of her face. She said, with a little gasp, 'Eliot!'

He said unsmilingly, 'Hello, Michelle,' and kept going.

'Eliot, wait a minute. I must speak to you.'

He sighed, then turned to face her. 'Not now,' he said gently.

'But I want to tell you how sorry I am. All those things in the papers. I was so humiliated...' Her voice tailed away breathlessly.

'I was sorry too,' he said levelly. 'Now, let's leave it at that. If Kevin sees you talking to me, there'll probably be a scene we'd both rather avoid.'

Natalie had been listening in bewilderment to this exchange, but suddenly it all made sense. In the stand, as they awaited the announcement that the horses had come under starter's orders, she said, 'That was Mrs Laidlaw, wasn't it?'

'Yes.' The firm mouth was grimly compressed.

It seemed safer not to ask any more questions, even if she'd been able to think of one, she thought ruefully. 'Are you still in love with each other?' was the most obvious, and the answer to that seemed equally clear. The encounter had been unexpected and painful for both of them. And somehow her own pleasure in the day had been diminished.

Even La Margarita's win by a short head wasn't the totally joyous event it should have been, although Eliot's relief was almost tangible.

'Is it as nerve-racking as being a jockey?' asked Natalie as they went down to the unsaddling enclosure.

'It's worse,' he said ruefully. 'When I rode, I had the trainer to blame if the horse didn't perform well. Now the buck stops here.' He glanced at her. 'I hoped you backed her?'

'Of course,' she said, and spoiled it by adding, 'Each way.'

'O ye of little faith!' But the teasing note was slightly off-key, as if his thoughts were elsewhere.

The Besants were overjoyed at their win, fussing La Margarita outrageously, and insisting that Eliot and Natalie join them in the bar for some champagne.

As they walked into the bar, she heard Eliot mutter, 'Oh hell!' half under his breath.

Kevin Laidlaw was there, standing a few yards away from them, and engaged in what was clearly a furious argument with a tall, heavily built man in a tweed overcoat.

'The joys of training,' Eliot observed laconically as they made their way to the Besants' table. 'If you win you get champagne. If you lose, you get the rough edge of the owner's tongue.'

'That was Terence Strang, the newspaper proprietor, wasn't it?' asked Natalie.

Eliot nodded, his face closed. 'Kevin trains his whole string—for jumping and the Flat,' he said.

'And you used to ride them?'

'At one time. But I'm glad I wasn't on any of them this afternoon. One fourth place, which should have been first, one faller, and a disappointing seventh. Not the kind of results Mr Strang would be looking for.'

'But even the best horses have their off days.' Natalie tried to be fair to Kevin Laidlaw, who was still having a very trying time, and under a great deal of public scrutiny.

'Sometimes off days can be habit-forming,' Eliot said meditatively.

The Besants were clearly more interested in celebrating than the rest of the programme, and after a few minutes Eliot excused himself to supervise the saddling of Likely Lad in the next race. Natalie hoped he would come back, but there was no sign of him, not even when the race was over with Likely Lad a promising second. Natalie thanked the Besants for their hospitality, and went in search of him. It was the last race of the day, and Wintersgarth had no runner in it. Natalie went down to the rails and looked around, as the horses cantered down to the start. Perhaps he'd gone to a put a bet on, she thought, or was waiting for her in the stand. She turned and was scanning the stand, shading her eyes with her card, when a hand fell on her arm and she looked round in surprise to see Kevin Laidlaw glaring at her.

'Where is he?' he demanded aggressively.

Natalie freed herself. 'I'm sorry?'

'Oh, don't play games with me,' he shot at her. 'You came with that bastard Lang—I saw you. And now you're on your own. So where is he?'

'I don't think that's any of your business.' Natalie began to walk away, but he grabbed her shoulder.

'On the contrary,' he almost hissed at her, 'it might be very much my bloody business!'

'Mr Laidlaw!' Natalie shook him off. 'People are looking at us.'

'How do you know who I am? Did he tell you?'

Natalie sighed. 'He didn't have to,' she said patiently. 'We've never met, but I'm Grantham Slater's daughter.'

'The devil you are!' He stared at her, then smiled offensively. 'Consolidating his position, is he? Making sure everything's sewn up nicely?'

Natalie winced away from the words, and the whisky fumes on his breath. She said curtly, 'Think what you like,' and took off through the crowd, dreading the possibility that he might follow her.

Judging by the state he was in, he'd probably spent the greater part of the meeting in the bar, she thought with distaste. No wonder Terence Strang had been so openly furious! She wondered if he'd always been a heavy drinker, or whether his drinking had been induced by professional stress—or some more personal problem. Like having an unfaithful wife...

She shut her mind to that. Whatever the reason, he was in an ugly mood, and maybe she should warn Eliot. She began to search methodically, and after five minutes she found him. He was standing in the shadows of the block housing the changing room and weighing-in facilities. He wasn't alone. Michelle Laidlaw was with him, and she was in tears.

Natalie halted abruptly, staring at them in shock. She heard Mrs Laidlaw say brokenly, 'Eliot, for God's sake have a little mercy!'

He returned flatly, 'It's impossible, and you know it.'

Natalie thought, I shouldn't be listening to this. She tried to retreat, but her unguarded movement attracted their attention, and they both turned and looked at her.

She saw Michelle Laidlaw clap both hands over her mouth in horror.

She heard herself say baldly, 'Your husband's looking for you, and he's drunk.' Then she turned and ran, leaving them together.

CHAPTER SIX

ELIOT caught her easily before she'd gone more than a few yards, his fingers digging into her arm as he seized her and pulled her round to face him.

'Where do you think you're going?' An angry muscle flickered beside his mouth.

'Anywhere,' she said jerkily, trying to pull away from him. 'Don't you think you'd better get back to your lady-love?'

'You don't know what you're talking about!'

'Oh, don't I?' She lifted her chin, furiously aware her voice was quivering. 'I'm not a chaperon. I'm the cover for your sordid affair with a married woman. Well, I hope her husband finds you—and knocks you senseless!'

'To hell with this!' His voice was molten with rage. 'I'm damned if I'm going to be condemned twice for the same offence—especially by you—and particularly as I'm not guilty anyway.'

His hand urged her forward, not gently. She twisted, looking for Michelle Laidlaw, but she'd disappeared. 'Leave me alone! Where are you taking me?'

'To the car park. You can sit in the car and calm down while I see the horses safely loaded. Then we'll talk.'

'There's nothing to talk about.'

'Oh, yes, there is, but if you don't want to talk, you can listen at least. And here's the first thing you can consider. The fact that Kevin's stinking drunk, and Michelle is weeping all over me has nothing to do with any non-existent love affair between us. It's because Terence

Strang is taking his horses away and sending them to us instead. So chew that over!'

Natalie sat in the Porsche, trembling with temper, staring through the windscreen. She felt like a naughty child, sent to her room. It was undoubtedly exactly what Eliot wanted her to feel. Well, if it was intended to make her more malleable, so she'd listen to any cock-and-bull explanation he chose to put forward, he would find he'd made a grave mistake.

When at last he came to join her, she didn't look at him, but continued to stare rigidly ahead of her.

He said, 'Are you prepared to listen to reason now?'

'Your reason?' she asked with bitter contempt. 'I'm not deaf, Eliot, or blind. I saw Michelle Laidlaw with you.'

He smiled grimly. 'Blind with prejudice where I'm concerned, wouldn't you say? I hope you're never called for jury service, Mrs Drummond. You're far too quick to pronounce sentence.'

She bit her lip. 'Well, say what you have to say, and let's get going.'

'Very well,' he said harshly. 'I repeat—I was never in love with Michelle Laidlaw, or she with me. And I never laid a finger on her while I was riding for her husband, or at any other time. And Kevin knows it.'

Natalie sent him a disbelieving look. 'Then why didn't he deny those stories when they appeared in the papers?'

'Because he preferred people to think I'd made a pass at Michelle and been kicked off the premises, than find out the real reason,' he said caustically. 'He probably started the rumours himself, as a cover story.'

'So what was the real explanation?'

Eliot was silent for a moment, his mouth compressed. Then he said, 'He wanted me to pull some horses for him.' He saw her startled look, and nodded. 'Yes, he wanted some races lost. He had financial problems, although he wouldn't specify what they were, and he thought he could persuade me to lose on the favourite so that he could back another runner at much better odds, and clean up.'

'And you wouldn't do it?'

'What do you think? I told him I wasn't prepared to risk an enquiry, and losing my licence—apart from the fact that there was no guarantee the other horse would win for him,' he added cynically. 'I reminded him that at the beginning of our association I'd told him I rode only to win. Anything else is unfair to the owner, and more than unfair to the horse. I said if he'd changed his mind about the rules of play, he could find another jockey, and I walked out.'

'And he—made up that story? But why?'

'To make sure if there was any mud-slinging, his handful would land first. He leaked the story somehow, then denied it in such a way everyone was convinced it had to be the truth. Anything I'd said after that would have looked like a lame attempt to save face.' He laughed harshly. 'And the mud stuck all right. Owners and trainers with attractive wives fought shy of me for quite a time, and that cost me financially—and emotionally as well.' His mouth twisted. 'I was living with someone. We'd begun to talk about the future—making it permanent. When the scandal broke, she couldn't wait to move out. She said there was no smoke without fire. So that was the end of that—and when the papers picked it up, it seemed to add the final confirmation of Kevin's story.'

The bitterness in his voice was authentic. He was telling the truth, Natalie thought with an odd pang.

She said, 'I'm—sorry that happened.'

'It was probably for the best. What relationship can work without trust?' He paused. 'But it's clear from what Terence Strang said today that Kevin's been using a more amenable jockey. And he's let too many of Strang's horses lose, today being the final straw. If that fall was genuine, I'm a Dutchman, although I don't suppose it can be proved.'

'And Terence Strang wants Wintersgarth to train his horses?' The full implication of what he had said earlier was just coming home to her.

Eliot smiled faintly. 'The jumpers to begin with, and maybe the others later.'

'Did you know he was going to be here?'

'I had a good idea he might be,' he said shortly. 'He rang me last week to ask my opinion on one of his horses I'd ridden as a two-year-old, and why it had developed all kinds of apparent faults since. It finished seventh today.' His mouth curled. 'He didn't tell Kevin he'd be coming to watch them run, otherwise the results might have been rather different.'

Natalie's thoughts were running ahead. She said, 'That's a lot of horses.'

He nodded. 'That's why we need those new boxes you've been so dubious about.'

'You—*knew* he'd send them to us?'

'I thought he would—unless Kevin came back to his senses.' He sighed. 'His financial problems are going to get a damned sight worse from now on, and that's why Michelle was pleading with me. She wanted me to persuade Strang to leave his horses with them.'

'But you couldn't do that...'

'As no doubt you heard me telling her,' he agreed, and she flushed.

'Yes,' she said in a subdued voice. 'I seem to have rather—jumped to conclusions.'

'And not for the first time.' There was a pause, then he said quietly, 'You really think I'm National Hunt racing's answer to Casanova, don't you?'

She said in a stifled tone, 'I don't think about it at all.'

'Liar,' he said softly. 'Every time a woman spoke to me this afternoon, I could see your mind working overtime, wondering whether I'd laid her.'

Her mouth tightened. 'You're not exactly an injured innocent in that respect—or no one would have believed Kevin Laidlaw.'

'I'm not a virgin,' he returned with a touch of mockery. 'But then you'd hardly expect me to be, at thirty-two. But I'm no sexual athlete either. If I'd really spent the amount of time in bed I'm credited with, I'd never have had the energy to win all those races.'

Her colour deepened. 'I really don't want to discuss this.'

'Then we'll change the subject.' Eliot started the engine. 'But if Kevin Laidlaw was looking for me, it was because I'd seduced his principal owner, not his wife. And now let's go and celebrate.' He smiled at her. 'I'll let you have the pleasure of telling Grantham about our latest acquisitions.'

Natalie returned his smile rather shyly. 'I'll phone him as soon as we get back.'

She had expected him to drive straight back to Wintersgarth, and was surprised when he pulled off the A1 and drove through the lanes to a large house standing in substantial grounds.

Natalie saw there were other cars parked outside. 'What is this place?'

'A restaurant. I told you—we're going to celebrate, beginning with dinner. I telephoned from the course to book a table.'

A day at the races was one thing, dinner *à deux* quite another, Natalie thought as he came round to open the passenger door.

She said, 'I'm not very hungry.'

'Then you can watch me eat,' said Eliot equably. 'Success always makes me ravenous. Now, are you getting out of the car, or do I have to carry you in there, cave-man style?'

It was said laughingly, but there was purpose in the hazel eyes, and Natalie scrambled out hastily, walking ahead of him with all the dignity she could command.

They sat at a lamplit table studying their menus. Natalie's had no prices, she noticed, wondering how Eliot had heard about this place. It was discreetly opulent, and clearly very expensive.

When they had given their orders to an attentive *maître d'hôtel*, Natalie excused herself and went to the powder-room to freshen up. She washed her hands, and deftly re-pinned a few errant strands of hair. She adjusted her lipstick, deciding as she studied herself that it was all that was strictly necessary. There was more colour in her cheeks than there had been for months, and an unaccustomed sparkle in her eyes. She shrugged off her suede jacket, shaking the creases from the sleeves of the cream silk shirt she wore beneath it, eyeing the effect critically in the mirror. She wished she'd had the opportunity to change, but it seemed she would have to go for a casual smartness instead. Her hand lifted and undid one of the shirt's tiny buttons, then moved down to the next, before she stopped short with a little gasp.

What on earth was she thinking of? she asked herself wildly. She'd never ever shown that much cleavage—not even when she'd been first married, and Tony had urged her to dress more daringly. God knows what Eliot would think if she went back to the table looking like this, she thought, her flush deepening painfully as she made haste to restore its usual decorum to her appearance.

When she made her way back to the table rather tensely, she found champagne on ice awaiting her.

She sank into her chair. 'You really mean to celebrate, don't you?'

Eliot grinned lazily. 'It's what we started on with the Besants. Why change a good habit?'

It was a wonderful meal, from the colourful chicken and pepper terrine which began it, to the sizzling lobsters in their wine and cream sauce. Afterwards, Eliot opted for cheese, while Natalie sampled out-of-season strawberries in a filigree pastry basket.

'I'm glad you recovered your appetite,' Eliot said silkily, as the waiter refilled their coffee cups.

Natalie sighed with happy repletion. 'It's a pity we can't do this every time a new owner sends us his horses,' she said dreamily, then blushed. 'I mean—I didn't mean...'

'Don't apologise.' Eliot reached across the table and took her fingers in his. 'I think it's a fantastic idea.'

He wasn't exerting the slightest pressure—she could have released herself at any time, and she knew it. Yet suddenly every inch of skin on her body seemed to be warning, tingling. Natalie stared down at the tablecloth, aware as never before of a strange, heated throb in her pulses.

She said in a choked voice, 'It's rather late. I think we should go.'

There was a pause, then Eliot nodded, and signalled to the waiter. Released, she clasped her hands together in her lap beneath the shelter of the cloth, willing the odd trembling to stop.

Wintersgarth was still a fair distance, she realised as she sat beside him in the car, in a darkness which seemed too enclosed, too intimate altogether. She touched the tip of her tongue to dry lips. If he was to stop the car in one of these lanes—and kiss her—there wouldn't be a great deal she could do about it.

But to her intense relief, he had no such intention. They were soon on the main road, and heading north again.

Indeed, rather to her surprise, they were back at the stables before she knew it. As he switched off the engine, Natalie said stiltedly, 'Thank you. That was—very nice.'

'It was indeed,' he said gravely. 'But it's not over yet. Come round the yard with me, and make sure everything's closed up for the night, then we'll have a nightcap.'

Natalie hesitated, every instinct warning her to refuse, but the thought of letting herself into the solitary darkness of the house wasn't particularly appealing, so she accompanied him silently as he went from box to box, checking their fastenings.

When he'd completed his rounds, she said rather breathlessly, 'I think I'd better go straight home—if you don't mind ...'

'One last drink,' he suggested. 'Then I'll walk you back to the house.'

She bit her lip. 'Well, just one.'

She stood in the russet-coloured sitting-room, feeling absurdly self-conscious, listening to the chink of glasses, and the smothered pop of a cork.

She gasped. 'You said—a drink,' she protested. 'Not more champagne!'

'It is a drink.' Eliot handed her the fizzing glass. 'It's not obligatory to finish the whole bottle, unless you want to.' He touched his glass to hers. 'Cheers.' Then he moved away to where the hi-fi was housed.

There was music in the air—not classics this time, but a woman's voice, husky and sensuous, and unfamiliar to Natalie.

'Who—who is that?' She sat primly down on one of the sofas, smoothing her skirt over her knees, relieved that Eliot had made no attempt to sit beside her.

'Carly Simon,' he said. 'Your musical education has been sadly neglected.'

She took a sip of her champagne. She thought, I could really get addicted to this stuff. Aloud she said, 'We didn't even have a record player in the house until Dad and Beattie were married. She says he's a Philistine, and proud of it.'

'And Tony wasn't interested either.'

She shook her head. 'Dad and he thought exactly alike—on a number of things.' She leaned back against the soft cushions, feeling relaxation spread through her like champagne bubbles. There was no fire in the grate tonight, but the heating was on, and the room was warm. It was strange, but she felt more comfortable in the flat now than she'd ever done when she lived there. She drank some more wine, closing her eyes and absorbing the music, letting that flow through her too, until she began to feel as if she was floating.

Eliot said softly, 'Come and dance with me.'

Her lashes lifted slowly. He was standing in front of her, smiling faintly as he looked down at her. He had discarded his jacket and tie, and unbuttoned his waistcoat. Her eyes widened as she saw he was still holding his glass.

'Aren't you going to put that down?'

He shook his head. 'It's only drinking and driving that's illegal. Drinking and dancing is fun. Try it.' He took her unresisting hand and drew her gently to her feet. 'You do dance?' His voice was teasing.

'I used to.' A lifetime ago, she thought, when I was someone else entirely. When I dreamed that love led to marriage, and happiness ever after.

It wasn't something, she discovered, that you forgot. The slow, sultry rhythm of the music captured her, and she began to move, shyly at first, but then with more confidence, humming the melody under her breath. Eliot matched her step for step, every sway of the hips, every turn of the body.

She held out her glass, and he refilled it, and she began to giggle.

'This is so silly.'

'And why not? Life's a pretty serious business most of the time.'

'That is true.' She drank some wine, tipping her head back ecstatically. 'Oh, that is so true.'

Eliot took her hand, and sent her spinning gently away from him, then drew her back again.

'Now that was clever,' she said solemnly.

'We're a gifted pair.' He ran a finger down her suede sleeve. 'Aren't you hot in this thing?'

'Terribly, but I have this problem with a glass.'

He took it from her fingers. 'Consider it solved.'

The buttons on her jacket were usually stubborn, but tonight they seemed to slide open. She wriggled her arms out of the sleeves, and dropped the jacket on to the sofa. *'Voilà!'*

He bowed slightly and handed back her glass, and they went on dancing. He made her spin round again, his hand on her waist, and she laughed, then sighed as the mood of the music changed and slowed.

Somehow, she'd finished the rest of the champagne, and Eliot took the empty glass from her and put it down, with his own. They stood facing each other, barely moving, then he reached forward, taking both her hands in his for a moment, then sliding his fingers up her silk-clad arms to her shoulders, and up again, stroking the side of her throat, and the sensitive area beneath her ears. Then his hands moved again, and Natalie realised he was taking the pins out of her hair. She felt the soft weight of it descend on the nape of her neck, and shook her head to free it properly.

'Mm,' he murmured in soft approval.

He clasped her waist lightly with both hands, drawing her forward a little so that their bodies were almost touching, but not quite. His fingers were warm and very strong through the silk that veiled her skin. His eyes were half closed as he looked at her, and she realised for the first time how long his lashes were. He seemed to be waiting for something—for her to touch him of her own volition, some instinct told her. And she needed to touch him because there was a warm, wild current running through her veins, and turning her legs to water. She put up her hands and clung to his shoulders, her eyes widening as she experienced their hard muscularity for the first time.

He bent his head, and she felt his lips gently touching her hair, then her forehead, brushing the soft concealing tendrils aside.

She was enclosed in a bubble of warmth and sensation, as his mouth trailed tantalisingly over her closed eyelids, and along her cheekbones, caressing the tip of her nose, the curve of her cheek, the point of her chin, but not her lips—never her lips, and it was killing her. She wanted to be kissed—needed it more than she needed air to breathe. Her hands clasped his neck, fingers locking as she drew him down to her.

There was no space between them any more. She was pressed against him, absorbing the hurry of his heartbeat, the sudden irregularity in his building through every pore, every nerve-ending in her own skin.

'Kiss me.' Had he said it, or was it her own potent unspoken longing she heard?

His tongue stroked her lips, parting them, then his mouth was on hers, moving softly at first, then more deeply, fuelling the strange aching need inside her in a sensual commingling of moist, urgent fire. She drank thirstily from that fire, answering it with her own.

When Eliot lifted his head, she moaned in disappointment.

'Oh, God,' he said hoarsely. 'My sweet...'

He poured a rain of tiny, burning kisses on her up-turned face, and her throat, while his hands moved with bewildering swiftness, releasing the buttons on her cuffs, then up to the shadowy vee at her throat, and down between the small, high breasts, uncovering her. She felt the shiver of silk on her skin as he pushed the shirt from her shoulders. The zip on her skirt rasped downwards, and she clung to him as he guided her out of the imprisoning fabric.

He went down on one knee to take off her long boots, ridding her almost casually of her tights as well. When he got to his feet again, she swayed towards him, the tips of her lace-covered breasts grazing the wall of his chest.

His hand twisted in her hair, tipping back her head, and he kissed her mouth again with a passion and a hunger that demanded appeasement. Her head was spinning, the race of her blood sounding like thunder in her ears. His fingers slid down her spine to find the small metal clasp which fastened her bra. He drew the straps down her arms, freeing her breasts from the concealing lace, covering the tumescent peaks with his hands, his fingers teasing the nipples into an agony of pleasure.

Was it the same for him? she wondered as her own hands found their way inside his shirt to begin a first, tentative exploration.

He kissed her as she caressed him, letting her know through the silent command of his mouth that he wanted more—much more from her. Trembling, she pulled and tore at his clothing, discovering him, adoring him with her hands, drawing a throaty groan of pleasure from him. He kissed her breasts, circling the hot, engorged peaks with his tongue, his hands stroking down her body, removing her underskirt and briefs as if he was brushing aside some gossamer cobweb.

He sank down on to the softness of the carpet, drawing her with him, his mouth locked hard to hers, his hand parting her thighs, the long fingers gentle, almost teasing as he caressed her, then, suddenly, not gentle at all.

She cried out as he entered her, pierced, transfixed by a pleasure so intense she thought she would die.

But she was alive, gloriously, superbly, shatteringly alive. Reborn, Natalie fell, entwined with him, into some nameless, endless void of delight.

CHAPTER SEVEN

NATALIE woke slowly in a room filled with sunlight, aware as she uncoiled herself of an incredible sense of well-being.

She hoped drowsily that it had nothing to do with the wildly erotic dreams which had assailed her during the night.

God knows what part of my subconscious they were dredged up from, she thought, half amused, half guilty, as she stretched languidly, and opened her eyes—to find it wasn't the autumn sun flooding between her own familiar curtains that gave that golden glow.

Not her room, she thought, dry-mouthed, her body freezing into swift rigidity. And, oh God, not her bed either.

Slowly, hardly daring to breathe, she turned her head.

Eliot had pushed the covers away during the night, and Natalie had an uninterrupted view of his tanned shoulders, and the long, naked length of his back. Every atom of air in her body seemed to be compressed into one stifled gasp of horrified disbelief.

No dream, she realised, as a burning blush of shame consumed her whole body. It had been all too real. She'd let Eliot Lang pour champagne down her as if it was going out of fashion, and then she—she'd ...

She pressed a clenched fist against her mouth. Memory was intruding now, reminding her remorselessly of everything that had happened the previous night.

And all she wanted to do was crawl away somewhere and die, before Eliot woke and saw her. Before he started remembering too...

He'd been drinking as well, she thought feverishly. If she—quietly slipped away, and later, when they inevitably encountered each other, she was her usual cool self, maybe—just maybe he'd think he'd been dreaming too. At least she could try.

She began to move with the utmost caution, edging her way gingerly to the edge of the bed, knowing even as she did so that it was all futile. That she should have made her escape hours before.

Because Eliot was awake. She watched him stir, stretch and turn, one arm already seeking her, lazily scooping her back across the bed to the warm curve of his body, as he smiled down into her outraged eyes.

'Good morning,' he said softly, and his hand lifted to cup her breast in a gesture of total familiarity. 'I don't think I remember a day which promised as much.'

Natalie said hoarsely, 'Let go of me. Let go of me now!'

The straight brows drew together as he studied her flushed face.

'Now why should I do any such thing?'

'Because I've got to go.' She tried to push away the caressing hand. 'I've got to get out of here now.'

'It's Sunday,' he reminded her. 'The horses don't go out to exercise today. We've hours before anyone starts wondering where we are.' He bent and kissed the bare curve of her shoulder, grimacing slightly as his stubble-roughened chin left a faint mark on her skin. 'I'll make a deal with you, darling. I'll shave, and you make some coffee, and we'll come back to bed and discuss our plans for the rest of the day.'

Natalie tried unavailingly to struggle free of his imprisoning arm. She said raggedly, 'You think I'd stay here with you—you utter bastard? You took advantage of me last night...'

He lifted himself on an elbow and stared down at her, brows lifting, the intimately teasing smile dying out of his eyes. He said slowly, 'There's a sweet old-fashioned expression.' He paused. 'Any advantage that was taken last night was utterly mutual, and you know it. Shall I show you the marks you left on me to prove it?' He began to push the sheet away, and Natalie shrank.

'No, just leave me alone. You're vile! You got me drunk—you know you did. You made me drink too much champagne, and then you—you...'

'Now you're being ridiculous.' His tone altered, became almost curt. 'All in all, I doubt whether you drank more than half a bottle during the entire twenty-four hours. Quite within your capacity, I'd have said, but enough to relax you sufficiently to forget a few of your damned inhibitions.' His gaze held hers. 'It wasn't just alcohol running through your bloodstream, sweetheart, but a healthy dose of sexual frustration. An equally potent additive, or didn't you know?'

'I don't want to know,' she said on a little anguished sob. 'I don't believe you. I—I've never behaved like this in my life before. Oh God, I've got to get out of here! I must have been crazy to trust you—to let you come anywhere near me. And now I'm going to feel dirty for the rest of my life!'

There was tension in him now, swift and dangerous.

'Why, thank you,' he said too courteously. 'Perhaps you should have considered that last night before falling into my arms quite so willingly.'

'I—I didn't!'

'Oh, yes, you did.' He smiled at her in insolent reminiscence. 'I always sensed, my lovely Natalie, that once the ice cracked, the spring floods would come roaring free, and how right I was! You were begging to be kissed—touched, but if you'd decided to call a halt at any point, I wouldn't have argued. It was you making the pace, lady, not me.'

'That isn't true!'

'Ah, but it is. And anyway, what's the problem?' He shrugged a shoulder. 'We were consenting adults, in private, and we wanted each other. It's not exactly a new situation.'

'Not for you.' Natalie's voice shook. 'Oh God, I wish I never had to see you again, you—you swine!'

'And you, my sweet, are a hypocrite—if we're calling names,' he retorted tersely. 'Why, even now...' He let his thumb brush slowly and insinuatingly across the quivering peak of her breast, bring the tender nipple to taut life. 'You see?'

Natalie bit on the inside of her lower lip until she could taste blood. 'I thought—I told you to let me go.'

'But I don't take orders from you, darling, either professionally or personally, remember?' He paused. 'Besides, your unflattering eagerness to leave suggests this may the only opportunity I'll ever have to enjoy you, so I may as well make the most of it.'

He moved, the lean body sliding over hers in explicit demand.

'You're disgusting!' Shock held her rigid beneath him.

'If you say so.' He sounded almost casual. 'In which case, I can dispense with the—er—usual preliminaries. Why don't you close your eyes, sweetheart, and think of something else—or someone else, if you prefer. Keep reminding yourself that Terence Strang is still sending us his horses—although I suppose you could blame that for your—downfall.' His breathing quickened. 'Ah, God, you feel so good. Why don't you relax that iron will of yours, and join me?'

She said, 'I'll see you in hell...' and stopped with a gasp, her body reacting swiftly and urgently to his invasion of her. Horrified and ashamed, she fought for control, for rejection, closing her heart, mind and senses to a possession which threatened to overwhelm her. And she won.

When, at last, his body shuddered violently into hers, she had not betrayed by a word or a movement the agony of need he had engendered within her.

'Thank you,' he said eventually, politely. 'It didn't compare with last night's performance, of course, but beggars can't be choosers.'

She said huskily, terrified that the savage, burning ache of desire inside her would become apparent in her face, 'May I go now? Have you—finished with me?'

Eliot lifted himself away from her. 'Yes—damn you!' There was a controlled violence in his voice which made her flinch.

She looked round the room. 'Where—where are my clothes, please?'

He shrugged shortly. 'In the other room, with mine. You have a convenient memory for details you prefer to forget.'

She swallowed. 'Well, would you mind—looking the other way?'

He sent her an incredulous glance, then started to laugh. 'Yes, I would mind,' he mocked. 'You've got a beautiful body, darling. I'm going to enjoy every last glimpse of it.'

Natalie's instinct was to run for the door, covering herself as best she could with her hands, but she knew that would only make her look and feel ridiculous.

She pushed back the covers and stood up, not even glancing at him, moving proudly, gracefully and unhurriedly, closing the bedroom door behind her.

But once she was safe from Eliot's appraising stare, she abandoned all pretence of dignity, almost flying to the sitting-room, wincing at the scatter of garments all over the carpet.

Her memory wasn't convenient at all. It was far too vivid, she thought, flinching from the sight of Eliot's elegant shirt with half the buttons torn from it, as she huddled into her own clothes. And the far from empty champagne bottle gave her no comfort either. His contradiction of her claim that she'd been drunk had a certain justice, she recognised wretchedly. She hadn't had that much, but it had gone straight to her head.

She shook her head, as she forced her feet into her boots. It wasn't the wine, she thought miserably. It was Eliot who'd gone to her head. She'd thought—all her previous experience suggested—that she was immune from sexual attraction. But now she knew very differently, and the realisation would haunt her for a long time.

She managed to leave the flat without anyone seeing her, and went straight to the office, where she typed her resignation and left it on Eliot's desk.

Then she went back to the house, and up to her room. She stripped, letting her clothes fall into an untidy pile. Presently, after she'd had a bath, she would fetch a plastic sack and bundle them into it. She never wanted to see any of them again—not even her boots, which were brand-new.

She soaked herself, immersed in hot water up to her chin, for nearly half an hour, then washed her hair, digging her fingers into her scalp.

It was a futile gesture, and she knew it, but she needed to do something which would make her feel like her own person again, instead of Eliot's possession—his plaything.

She was on edge for the rest of the day, watching the path that led to the front door, half expecting his arrival, his invasion of her privacy.

But she was left severely alone. At lunch time, she cooked and forced down some leathery scrambled eggs, and, when evening came, she hunted through the freezer for a single portion of one of Beattie's delicious casseroles, although she did it less than justice.

She tried to catch up on some reading, and when that palled, to watch television, but she couldn't relax, or prevent her mind turning relentlessly back to the events of the past twenty-four hours. She kept finding the image of them being slowly and relentlessly re-created across her aching mind.

It was so totally out of character, she wailed inwardly. Her brief experience of married life had taught her quite unequivocally that sexual matters left her cold. Her wedding night had been painful, both physically and emotionally, and matters between Tony and herself had never improved. She'd been alarmed and revolted by his insistence on enforcing his rights, in spite of her shrinking. She'd believed she was incapable of the response he'd demanded, in some way incomplete as a woman.

'It's like making love to a bloody waxwork!' Tony's voice, bitter with disillusion, came back to her over the years, and she shivered, wrapping her arms defensively round her body.

So how could she possibly have wanted—have encouraged Eliot to do those things to her?

She must have been mad, she thought, and now she had to live with the humiliation of it.

She tried to make some plans. She had a few savings, so she could afford to support herself while she looked round for work. But not locally, she thought. She would get as far away from Wintersgarth as it was possible to go without falling off the edge of the world.

And she would have to find some convincing story to reconcile Grantham to what he would undoubtedly see as her defection, she thought, biting her lip. A clash of personalities? Or irreconcilable differences, as they said in divorce cases. But would her father accept that—and would Beattie's shrewd eyes see through it?

She groaned to herself. Why hadn't she listened to the warning voice in her head last night and come back here, decorously and alone? She would have been spared all this—dissimulation.

And she would also, she realised, as the dark hours wore on, have been spared the misery of physical frustration which, for the first time in her life, kept her tossing and turning in heated restlessness for most of the night.

She put on a black skirt and a matching sweater, shapeless and elderly, with the sole merit of buttoning high to the throat, the following morning, and scraped her hair back into an elastic band at the nape of her neck before going down to the office.

She was early, but Eliot was there before her, waiting for her, his dark brows drawn together, his mouth set in an uncompromising line.

'I got your letter.' He held it up between finger and thumb as if it was distasteful, then tore it across and dripped the pieces into the waste-basket.

'That's an empty gesture.' Natalie faced him, keeping her voice steady with an effort. 'I'm leaving anyway, at the end of the week.'

He shook his head. 'You're paid a salary. I think that entitles us to a month's notice, and I'm sure that will be your father's view as well.' He paused. 'As a matter of interest, how do you intend to justify your departure?'

She said tautly, 'I'll think of something.'

'Why not try the truth?' The hazel eyes bored relentlessly into her pale face. 'That having enjoyed yourself with me all night, you started hating yourself in the morning.'

'Isn't it bad enough for me to know what I did?' she asked wearily. 'Do you really think I'd hurt Grantham by letting him know I'd behaved like a slut?'

'Is that how you regard yourself?' There was an odd note in his voice. 'It's a hard judgement for letting yourself be human for once.'

'You make it sound so simple!'

'Because it isn't that complicated.' Eliot took a step towards her, halting, his frown deepening incredulously as Natalie backed away. 'My God!' He flung up a hand. 'All right, I'll keep my distance. But I want you to know, Natalie, that I don't regret a thing that happened the other night, and you shouldn't either.' His mouth twisted. 'The aftermath wasn't particularly admirable, perhaps, but your hysterical assertions that I'd made you drunk and forced myself on you got under my skin.

Anyway, running away—either from me, or from yourself—won't solve anything.'

'You can't stop me,' Natalie averred unevenly.

'No, but when Grantham asks me why you're leaving, as he assuredly will, I can tell him.' He paused. 'I don't think he'd be as shocked or as upset as you think. He might even see it as a way of cementing our partnership for good and all.'

It was like a nightmare repeating itself.

She said hoarsely, 'No. You've made your contract with Grantham—and I'm not part of the deal.' Dear God, not again. Not this time.

What the hell do you think I'm suggesting?' he asked harshly. 'Some bloody dotted line, with you on it?'

She shrugged. 'It's been done before.' And to me, she wanted to scream. *And to me.*

Eliot was silent for a time, then he said, 'OK, forget I ever mentioned it. The deal is this—you stay here in return for my silence. Because while it wouldn't cause Grantham any great grief to know I'd seduced you, it would hurt him deeply to see you walk away.' He paused. 'And I'll play my part, Natalie. I'll make a conscious effort not to touch you, or—intrude upon your personal space in any way. Will that satisfy you? The other night is—closed, finished, forgotten. A temporary aberration on both sides.' He looked at her watchfully. 'Well, shall we declare a truce—for Grantham's sake?'

Natalie said in a muffled voice, 'I don't seem to have a great deal of choice.' She moved behind her desk and sat down. 'Do you have anything else to say, because I have work to do—and I'd rather like to be alone.'

His glance was cynical. 'What you'd really like is for me to vanish from the face of the earth.' He shook his head. 'I'm not prepared to oblige you that far, but I'll guarantee to keep out of your way as much as I can. And Grantham will be back later today, which will release you from my exclusive company anyway.' He went out of the office, closing the door behind him.

She watched his tall figure cross the yard and go under the arch, then she slumped into her chair, hands shaking, body trembling.

She felt as if she'd been reprieved. She knew only too well—she'd known from the beginning what Grantham was hoping for. In this very office, that first day, he'd been none too subtle about it.

He might huff and puff, but he would be secretly delighted if he learned that Eliot and herself were involved in an intimate relationship—would insist righteously on it being legalised...

Her mind closed, wincing, against the prospect. She'd already been locked into one marriage with a man who cared more for the main chance than he'd done for her, although she hadn't realised it at first. But she couldn't allow it to happen again, because this time she wouldn't have a single illusion to sustain her. Marriage to her would simply increase Eliot's share, his control of Wintersgarth. Grantham might have barred her from the running of the stables, but she was still his heiress. And she was no longer the starry-eyed innocent who believed such things didn't matter.

It was what Tony had married her for, after all, she thought wearily. He'd put on a good act for a while, until he became too bored to bother any more.

And herself? Well, she'd been carried away by his boyish good looks, by the glamour that he was a rising star of National Hunt racing. But had she really loved him any more than he'd loved her? Wouldn't she have found some way of overcoming her aversion to his sexual advances, if she had loved him? And wouldn't it have been more than her pride that was hurt when she eventually found out about his infidelities?

For three years now, she'd kept all these questions locked away at the back of her mind. Now Eliot had released them, opened her own private Pandora's box to scrutiny.

Suddenly everything had changed, she thought. And in spite of his assurances, nothing would ever be simple again.

'Natalie, come and look at this horse.' The sound of her father's voice from the doorway made her start guiltily and thrust the letter she'd been reading back into its envelope, and back into concealment amongst the pile of mail in front of her.

She got to her feet. 'Another delivery from Mr Strang?' Over the past seven weeks, the new extension had been finished, and the horses had been arriving. Their transfer had caused a lot of comment and speculation in the sporting papers, and it was widely rumoured that Kevin Laidlaw might be declaring himself bankrupt before too long.

'Ay, his latest acquisition, the big, awkward devil.'

In spite of her inner preoccupations, Natalie couldn't help wondering whether Grantham was referring to the animal or its owner.

'What's the matter with it?' She followed him into the yard and under the arch to where the lads were gathered in a semi-circle around a horse box.

'Just about everything. The previous owner bred the colt himself. He had a son who wanted to ride as an amateur, it seems.' Grantham shook his head in disapproval. 'But he didn't know how to break it properly, and it was too much for the lad, so they put it up for sale, and one of Strang's agents bought it. And now we have to cope with the result,' he added with obvious relish. 'It tried to kick its way out of the box before we could get the back down, and then it nearly bit a chunk out of young Micky. Eliot's with it now, trying to calm it down.'

Natalie's body clenched in swift automatic reaction. 'Oh.' She turned away with an ostentatious shiver. 'It's rather too chilly this morning to stand about watching Mr Lang be his usual brilliant self. Tell me when it's over.' She turned away, ignoring the look of disfavour Grantham sent her, and began to make her way back to the office, but a shrilly enraged whinny and a sudden plunging of hooves made her swing back again, in spite of herself. Hidden by the archway, she watched dry-mouthed as Eliot coaxed his wild-eyed sweating charge down the ramp into the yard. Midstream clearly didn't like his new surroundings, or the silent audience awaiting him, because he lashed out vigorously with his back legs, with Eliot hanging on to him, nothing in his face or attitude to suggest he found this behaviour in any way untoward.

'There's gipsy somewhere in the lad's genes,' Grantham had said more than once, and Natalie knew what he meant. It was no wonder he'd been able to get the best out of so many of his horses, on his way to becoming champion jockey, she thought, as she watched Midstream circling restively. He seemed to cast some kind of spell on even the most bad-tempered and recalcitrant mounts. When Midstream rode out to exercise, she knew exactly who would be on his back.

She stayed, peeping round the wall until the rearing and plunging animal began to subside, and Eliot turned him to lead him to his new stable. She despised herself for hiding round corners like this, but she had to admit Eliot had kept to his pledge, betraying by neither word nor look that they'd ever exchanged more than the common courtesies. And she'd done her best to play along with that too, which meant that forming part of an admiring crowd when he was exercising his gifts on a new and excitable horse was strictly taboo.

As soon as Midstream was safely bestowed, Eliot would be wanting coffee for himself, and the driver of the box, and the lad who had travelled with the horse— although a lot of good he'd been, Natalie thought caustically, as she filled the new coffee machine and switched it on.

She was on her way back to her desk when the telephone rang.

It was a woman's voice, collected and businesslike. She was ringing, she announced, on behalf of Miss Oriel Prince.

'I understand you have two of her horses in training,' she went on. 'Miss Prince plans to visit them when she returns to Britain in a fortnight's time. I presume this is in order?'

'Perfectly.' Natalie grimaced at the receiver. Owners visited all the time, and were generally welcome, but Sharon with open dismay had been predicting this descent since the newspapers had announced that Oriel Prince had signed a contract to make a mini-series for television in the near future.

'Why couldn't she have stayed in America?' Sharon had grumbled. 'It's not the horses she's coming to see anyway,' she added. 'She doesn't give a damn for them, except when they win for her.'

Natalie had murmured something non-committal and turned away, aware this was the kind of discussion it was unwise to get involved in.

The woman's voice had taken on a trace of uncertainty. 'Wintersgarth—where is that precisely?' Natalie gave patient directions, which were clearly being written down at the other end. When she'd finished, the other woman said with patent disapproval, 'It's a very long way from London.'

'A lot of places are,' Natalie agreed levelly.

She had replaced the receiver, and made a note of the projected date of Miss Prince's visit in the diary kept for the purpose, when Eliot walked in.

'The coffee's nearly ready.' She kept the usual neutrality in her voice, and avoided looking at him directly.

'Thank you.' He sat down. 'Can you check when that damned Micky had his last anti-tetanus. He claims he can't remember.'

'In that case, he probably needs a booster. He hates injections.' She walked towards the table in the corner, where the paraphernalia for coffee-making was set out. The aroma of the freshly-percolated brew was filling the air, and Natalie found she was wrinkling her nose as she assembled the cups, trying consciously not to breathe in. She'd never noticed before what a nauseating smell coffee had. And on the thought there was a sudden lurch in her stomach, a bitterness in her throat, and gagging, she ran for the tiny washroom.

She just made it to the basin, her hands clutching its cool porcelain as she retched weakly over and over again. In the middle of it, with a kind of embarrassed horror, she realised Eliot was beside her.

'Go away,' she managed, before another paroxysm intervened.

'Presently.' He ran the cold tap on to his handkerchief, wrung it out, then gently wiped her forehead and lips, as she clung shivering to the basin.

He said, 'Don't move. I'll get you a chair.'

She wanted to protest, but it was altogether easier to accede, and she was thankful to sit down. Her legs seemed to have been transformed into jelly, and her head felt as if it didn't belong to her. She was aware of Eliot wiping her face again, then he left the washroom, closing the door, and leaving her gratefully in peace. She could hear voices in the office, and could only be thankful they hadn't arrived a few minutes sooner.

The next time the door opened Beattie was gazing at her, her face twisted with concern. 'My dearest girl! What is it?'

Natalie shook her had, wincing. 'Something I ate, I expect. I feel all right now.'

'It's more likely to be a virus.' Beattie surveyed her with misgiving. 'You look like a ghost. Anyway, you're coming home with me to lie down. Oh yes, you are, my girl.' Firmly she stifled Natalie's protest. 'The boss's orders. And if you're no better tomorrow, I'll get Doctor Bishop.'

'I'll be fine tomorrow. I'm fine now,' Natalie said desperately. 'And I have things to do. I've hardly started on the morning mail and...'

Beattie said something vulgarly and cheerfully dismissive about the morning mail. She put an arm round her stepdaughter and lifted her tenderly to her feet.

As they reached the office door, Natalie tried to hang back. 'I really ought to...'

'Later,' said Beattie, and meant it.

In spite of her inner misgivings, Natalie found it pleasant to be tucked up as if she was a little girl, with a hot water bottle. Later Grantham came in to see her, walking gingerly as if approaching a deathbed.

'I thought there was something up when you moaned about the cold.' He frowned at her. 'It's not like you to be ill.'

'I'm not ill.' She smiled at him, recognising the concern under his words. 'I feel a total fraud lying here.'

'Well, Beattie says you've to stay where you are,' he said, and that settled the matter.

When he'd gone, Natalie lay staring at the ceiling, her mind beginning its journey on a new and frightening treadmill. Eventually she dozed, and when she opened her eyes, found Eliot standing by the bed, looking down at her, his face expressionless.

'How are you?' he asked quietly.

'I'm fine.' In spite of the fact that she was wearing a long-sleeved, high-necked print nightgown, Natalie had to resist an urge to draw the covers up to her chin. 'It—it was just a passing thing.'

'I doubt it.' He sat down on the edge of the bed, his eyes never leaving her face. 'Morning sickness in pregnancy rarely passes as easily as that.' He reached into his pocket, and took out the letter she'd been reading earlier, tossing it on to the bed between them. 'Or was the result of your test going to be your little secret?'

CHAPTER EIGHT

THERE was a long and terrible silence.

'Well, answer me,' said Eliot. 'Did you have any intention of telling me I was going to be a father?'

Natalie found a voice from somewhere. 'How—how dare you read my letter?'

He shrugged. 'I didn't mean to. I thought I'd help out by going through the correspondence and dealing with anything vital.' He flicked the envelope with his finger. 'This—was amongst it all, and I read it before I realised what it was.' His face was unsmiling. 'And when I did realise, the ethics of the situation became irrelevant. Now, will you answer my question. Were you going to tell me?'

She said huskily, 'No—no, I wasn't.'

His brows lifted. 'You didn't think I'd find it of marginal interest to learn you were carrying my child?'

Her chin jutted defiantly. 'To use your own words—the ethics of the situation became irrelevant. Anyway, how do you know it's yours?'

His voice was icy. 'Oh, stop pretending, Natalie! A girl who was as shy and virginal in her responses as you were that first time with me doesn't sleep around. And your reaction afterwards did not, frankly, suggest you were going to leap out and grab the first man you saw, so that you could compare notes about us.'

She bit her lip. 'Well, it doesn't matter. It makes no real difference.'

'I'd have said it made one hell of a lot of difference.'

She shook her head. 'It's my problem. I'll deal with it. I'll think of something.'

There was another silence, then he said carefully, 'By "something", I hope you don't mean an abortion.'

Her mind winced away in shock from the ugliness of the word. No, something screamed in her mind. *Not that—never that* ...

She didn't meet his gaze. 'I suppose—it's a possibility.'

She wanted him to go—to leave her to think. Her mind refused to work properly while he was standing over her, like judge and accuser in one.

'You seem to have everything all worked out,' Eliot observed at last. 'If that's what you're considering, I can see why you weren't too concerned about the morning sickness.'

Natalie was feeling sick again, but the cause wasn't physical. He thought—he really thought she was capable of contemplating such a thing.

'I can explain the sickness away as food poisoning or a virus,' she said quietly. 'And you don't have to be concerned either. That—incident is still closed, finished and forgotten. Nothing changes that.'

'All neat and tidy,' Eliot remarked shortly. He got to his feet. 'But I hope at least you'll let me help with any necessary arrangements. It's the least I can do in the circumstances.'

'There's really no need.' Natalie turned on to her side, away from him, as if settling herself for sleep. 'I'm just sorry you had to find out.'

When she heard the bedroom door close behind him, the breath was expelled from her taut body in an enormous sigh of relief.

He'd looked very odd, strained and pale, she thought, punching at her pillow to make it more comfortable. Was this actually the first time one of his sexual encounters had ended in an unwanted pregnancy? Surely not.

She closed her eyes wearily. Certainly he'd spoken about the possibility of her—getting rid of the baby very calmly.

She laid a hand gently, protectively over her abdomen. Because it was a baby—a small human being, and not merely proof, if proof were needed, of how ruinous a night's casual sex could be.

Ever since she'd missed her first, regular period, she'd tried to tell herself it couldn't be true. That her sensible, well-ordered life couldn't have plunged into chaos because of one bitterly regretted night. But nature wasn't interested in the whys and wherefores of lovemaking, she thought, or in subsequent regrets, however sincere—only in the continuation of the species.

She sat up, pushing her hair back from her face. It was no good lying here, imagining she was going to get some sleep. She was far too on edge to rest. She might as well get dressed, she thought, and go down to the office. Apart from anything else, she needed to make an appointment with the doctor, to check on her general health.

She glanced down at the coverlet, and stiffened. The letter—her letter—about the pregnancy test wasn't there. Yet she'd seen Eliot put it down on the bed. She moved the covers, hunting for it, and looked on the floor, but there was no sign of it.

Perhaps he'd taken it with him inadvertently, she thought, and bit her lip. Eliot rarely did things inadvertently.

She threw back the covers and got out of bed, dressing hastily in jeans and a high-necked sweater. She had difficulty with the zip on her jeans and looked down at herself with disquiet. Already, it seemed, her body was changing, adapting to its new occupant.

She ran downstairs into the hall, just as the drawing-room door opened and Beattie emerged, laughing. She saw Natalie and her smile widened. 'You're up,' she said with pleasure. She called back into the room, 'Grantham, she's here!' She put her arm round Natalie's unresisting waist and drew her into the room. 'Darling, we're so happy for you. So delighted for you both.'

Natalie gave her a confused look. 'I don't understand,' she began, and stopped dead as she saw Eliot, lounging on the windowseat.

Her father got up from his chair. 'So, what's this I'm hearing about you, my lass? Going to make me a grandfather at last, are you?' He put his arms round her and hugged her. He said fondly, 'I suppose I should be angry with you both—come the heavy father. But you're not the first couple to enjoy your honeymoon before the wedding, and you won't be the last, I dare say. Now, sit down, girl, sit down.'

She was thankful to feel the edge of the sofa beneath her before she collapsed.

She said, 'Will someone tell me what's been going on?'

Beattie said gaily, 'I suppose it was awful of us to start talking wedding plans without you, darling, but we're all so excited, we couldn't help ourselves.'

'Excited?' Natalie's voice sounded hollow. She looked up, met Eliot's enigmatic look across the room. She said, on a little sigh, 'You—told them?'

'Well, of course he told us,' Grantham broke in impatiently. 'It was the honourable thing to do, after all. And I agree with him that you should get married as soon as possible—a special licence job, if you have to.

There are still people round here who count on their fingers between the wedding and the christening.'

Beattie said eagerly, 'I can easily manage the reception here. Eliot said you both wanted a very quiet affair, with just family.'

'Did he?' Perhaps she'd fallen asleep after all, and was having a nightmare, she thought numbly. She couldn't really be sitting here, listening to her marriage to Eliot Lang being discussed as if it was a *fait accompli*.

He'd been too quiet, too calm during their conversation in the bedroom, she realised now. He must have come straight downstairs and told them about the baby. He knew—everyone knew—how Grantham felt, how he wanted a grandson to carry on his heritage at the stables. And Eliot had traded on that ruthlessly. Because now that Grantham knew about the baby any hope of vanishing for the next year, and having the baby adopted at the end of it, was out of the question.

She was in a trap, she thought feverishly, and the walls were closing in on her.

Beattie said sharply, 'Natalie, are you sure you should have got up so soon? You've gone very white again.'

Eliot rose to his feet. He said, 'She's been under a lot of stress. I'll take her back to her room.'

As he came towards her, Natalie put up a hand to ward him off, tried to speak, but no sound came. Eliot lifted her bodily off the sofa into his arms and carried her to the door.

Grantham said, 'Mind how you go, lad. She's doubly precious to me now.'

'And to me,' said Eliot.

As he carried her upstairs, she said thickly, 'You—bastard. You devious, conniving bastard!'

'Actually, I was born in wedlock,' he said flatly. 'And I intend my child shall be too. That's what this is all about.' He shouldered his way into her bedroom and dropped her on to the bed almost negligently, his face grim as he looked at her.

He said, 'Now, you're going to listen to me, you self-centered little bitch. That's my child you have inside you, not some insignificant piece of garbage you can have—scraped out of you, and forget about. You're not thinking clearly, Natalie. You're panicking, running for cover, and you don't care who you hurt in the process. Well, there are other people involved in any decision about this baby—and even if you reject the notion that I might have some say in the matter as the baby's father, you can't be cruel enough to ignore Grantham's feelings, Grantham's hopes. Or could you?'

She wanted to scream at him, to deny totally and finally the idea that she could ever have had the pregnancy terminated. Instead, she said in a stifled voice, 'But it doesn't have to be—marriage. I could go away somewhere—even keep the baby afterwards...'

'With me supplying maintenance and allowed the occasional visit, I suppose.' Eliot was very white under his tan. He paused. 'Is it marriage in general you're opposed to—or marriage to me in particular?'

She bit her lip. 'Marriage—in general.'

He said, 'Is Drummond's memory still so potent with you, then? I hadn't thought...' He was silent for a few moments. Then he said, rather more curtly, 'As it happens, this isn't the way I'd have chosen to embark on married life either, but the choice is out of our hands. The baby exists, and I don't think, moral grounds aside, that you're emotionally or rationally equipped to cope with an abortion. It isn't an ideal world, Natalie. People are having to compromise all the time, and we probably are no worse off than thousands of other couples. In fact, we have an advantage, because I really want to care for you, and the child. Can't you settle for that?'

She said wearily, 'As you say, the choice is out of our hands now. Make what arrangements seem best.'

Her chest and throat felt tight, and tears were stinging unexpectedly behind her eyes. She was afraid of breaking down in front of him, afraid of the comfort he might feel obliged to offer.

Huskily, she said, 'Will you go now, please. After all, you've got what you wanted.'

'Have I?' he said. 'How interesting that you should think so.'

Eyes closed, Natalie sensed his movement away from her, heard the bedroom door close, and pressed her clenched fist convulsively against her trembling lips to force back the wrenching sob rising inside her.

Compromise, she thought. Her entire life seemed to have been based on it so far, and this time would be the bitterest of all.

They were married just under a fortnight later. Natalie had expected a brief ceremony in front of the registrar, but Eliot had insisted on the local church. His parents would expect it, he told her flatly.

Natalie had looked back at him, almost dazedly. She'd been too taken up with her own problems, her own heart-searchings, to consider that she was being drawn into a new and extended family.

His smile was twisted. 'It's all right, they won't eat you! My mother's dream has been to have me out of racing and settled with a family.'

'Do they know about the baby?'

'Yes. They asked, and I saw no point in lying. And they realised years ago that I was never going to live my life in the orderly, respectable sequence they wanted, so they weren't that shocked.' He smiled faintly. 'Like Grantham, they feel that a grandchild in prospect outweighs all other considerations.' He paused. 'However, I did give them the impression that we'd fallen madly in love, and been totally carried away by our feelings.' He saw her wince, and nodded grimly. 'So, if you could manage to dump your usual expression of having a shotgun held against your head, I'd be grateful.'

Natalie looked down at her folded hands. 'I'll do my best.'

And she did. She kept a radiant smile so firmly anchored to her face that her muscles ached with the effort. And no one could fault her appearance either, she told herself. The cream silk suit she'd found in a Harrogate boutique looked exactly right, even if Beattie had lifted a disapproving eyebrow at the jade silk blouse worn beneath it, and the matching trim on Natalie's wide-brimmed cream hat.

'Green's supposed to be unlucky at weddings.'

Natalie shrugged. 'I'm not superstitious.'

As the racing season was in full swung, and the stables committed up to the hilt, she had presumed that after the wedding life would go on as usual. But she discovered that Eliot had booked them in for a couple of days at an old-fashioned country hotel, sheltering beneath a fell in the Lake District.

It wasn't a honeymoon, she told herself firmly. More— a breathing space before she had to move back into the flat. Because that was where they'd be living, as Eliot had made clear.

'There are no ghosts.' The hazel eyes had met hers, directly, almost challengingly.

'No,' she admitted quietly. Only, she thought, the ghost of an unhappy girl watching her dreams fall into fragments around her. Only the haunting memory of her failure as a woman and a wife.

And those she carried within her.

The send-off from the reception was a muted affair compared to the last occasion, Natalie thought. When she'd left with Tony, there'd been old shoes and tin cans clanking from the back of the car hired to take them to the airport, and the driver had grumbled that they'd be late as he struggled to remove them. It had been a breakneck drive, too, with Tony still pallid from his stag night. At the time, she had felt an odd hurt that he'd seemed to need to get so very drunk in order to face marrying her. He'd been ill on the flight to Malaga too, and on their arrival at the hotel in Marbella he had insisted, in spite of Natalie's fatigue and hunger, that they go straight to bed.

Even now the memory had the power to make her cringe, physically and emotionally.

She shot a nervous sideways glance at Eliot as he drove. Apart from exchanging their marriage vows, they had hardly said more than half a dozen words to each other all day. And apart from asking politely if she was warm enough, and if she wanted some taped music, he was making no effort to engage her in conversation now.

She wondered what was occupying his thoughts. Perhaps he was thinking of the girl he had once planned to marry, who had thrown him over because of the Laidlaw scandal. Maybe the fact that he'd already loved and lost made it easier for him to accept second best with her, she thought with an odd pang.

The sun was already setting when they arrived at their destination. Natalie caught her breath as Eliot helped her from the car. It was a very old building, white-washed on the outside, and heavily beamed with stone-flagged floors inside.

Their room was at the side, with an uninterrupted view through a gap in the bare trees to the lake. Natalie walked to the window, and stared out as if fascinated by her surroundings. Anything, she thought with a kind of des-peration, to keep her from considering the implications of the big four-poster bed, with its pretty chintz canopy and coverlet, which dominated the room. The whole room had an air of old-fashioned comfort, from the solid, polished furniture to the fire burning in the grate, although the adjoining bathroom made no such con-cessions to the past in its gleaming modernity.

She listened to Eliot thanking the porter who had brought up their luggage, and adding the appropriate tip. Then the door closed, and they were alone.

She could feel tension spreading through her, turning her rigid.

'God, I want you, Nat,' Tony had mumbled. He hadn't even bothered to undress properly. She remembered his weight on her, the desperate thrusting into her unpre-pared, unaroused flesh.

Eliot said from just behind her, 'Why don't we leave the unpacking until later?'

Her hands gripped the windowsill, the knuckles white. 'I—I'd rather unpack now.'

'As you wish.' He sounded faintly surprised. 'I thought maybe you'd prefer to have some tea in the lounge, and go for a walk before dinner.'

'Oh—yes.' She gestured at the silk suit. 'But I'll need to put something warmer on.'

'Fine,' he said equably. 'I'll wait for you downstairs. Do you simply want tea, or can you manage a sandwich?'

She shook her head. 'No—nothing to eat, thanks,' she managed.

He nodded, watching her quizzically. He said, 'Relax, sweetheart. You don't have to put on an act for our respective families any more. Now, I'll go and order that tea.'

By herself, Natalie opened her case and hung her things away in the cavernous wardrobe. She bit her lip over the last items—the white chiffon nightgown, misted with hyacinth blue flowers, and matching peignoir, which Beattie had insisted on.

'You're not wearing brushed nylon or winceyette on honeymoon,' she'd vetoed firmly.

Natalie hesitated for a moment, then unpacked Eliot's case too. No pyjamas, she noted, in any fabric. No doubt he was remembering the night when he'd made her—behave like an animal, and was hoping for a repetition. Well, he would soon discover his mistake, she thought, sending a speculative glance at the Victorian chaise-longue, upholstered in the same chintz as the bed which stood near the window. It was intended for purely decorative purposes, she knew, but it could be put to practical use as well.

She changed into a simple pleated skirt in russet tweed, topped it with a high-necked cream sweater, and, draping a casual jacket over her arm, went downstairs.

'You didn't eat much,' Eliot commented critically later as they made their way into the lounge for after-dinner coffee. 'Are you feeling sick again?'

Natalie flushed, shaking her head. 'It only happens occasionally. I'm very lucky, really. I—I suppose I'm tired. Today's been rather a strain.'

'Then we'll have an early night,' he said pleasantly, as he guided her to a table not far from the blazing log fire on the wide hearth.

She hung back. 'Would you mind if I went up now? I don't think I really want coffee.'

'If that's what you wish.' He shot her a swift glance. 'You don't object if I have some?'

'Oh, no.' Her response had been too quick and too vehement, she thought vexedly as his mouth twisted in sardonic acknowledgement. Eliot took the key from his pocket and dropped it into her hand.

'I'll join you presently,' he said lightly. 'Don't forget and lock the door before you go to sleep, will you?'

Natalie sent him a weak smile in return, but her heart was beating rapidly, as she went up the stairs. The glitter in the hazel eyes had warned her quite succinctly that he was capable of summoning the manager with a master key, if necessary.

There were plenty of extra blankets in the wardrobe, and she made up the chaise-longue as comfortably as possible, adding one of the fat, lace-trimmed pillows from the bed.

Then she undressed, put on the new nightgown and peignoir, and sat down nervously on the edge of the bed to await her bridegroom.

True to his word, Eliot didn't keep her waiting long.

He closed the door behind him quietly and leaned against it for a moment, his eyes roving over her in unmasked appreciation of the picture she presented in the cloud of chiffon, her copper hair loose on her shoulders.

Then his gaze went past her to the makeshift bed by the window, and she saw him stiffen. He had gone very pale, she saw, and a muscle flickered beside his mouth.

She braced herself for an explosion.

He said quietly, 'I went into this marriage in good faith, Natalie. I meant what I said about wanting to protect you, and the baby. But I never at any time intended it to be less than a real marriage.'

Her mouth was dry. She said, 'I—we shouldn't... The doctors say there can be a risk so early on.'

'I'm not unaware of that,' he said bleakly. 'Believe it or not, I never intended to spend our time here in some non-stop sexual marathon. But I expected one of the few perquisites of this marriage to be my wife's presence at night in my bed, in my arms.' He walked across and sat down beside her, taking her cold hands in his. He said gently, 'Sweetheart, this is no way to begin. Sleep with me tonight—please.'

His fingers were strong and very warm as they held hers. She had a sudden vivid memory of those same fingers stroking her body, caressing her to some inexplicable madness, and her eyes dilated in panic.

She tore free from his clasp. 'No—I can't. I won't!'

Eliot stared at her for a moment, then he shrugged and got to his feet, taking off his jacket and beginning to loosen his tie. He said without visible emotion, 'Very well. But I hope that couch is softer than it looks. I'd hate for it to give you backache in your delicate condition.'

It was the last reaction Natalie had expected, and she felt her jaw drop.

She said stupidly, 'Me? But I thought you...'

'Then you're under a misapprehension, my sweet.' He began to unbutton his shirt. 'I intend to pass my wedding night in comfort, not squirming around on a piece of furniture designed for a miniature version of Quasimodo. Naturally, you're still welcome to join me, if you wish,' he added casually.

He smiled at her as he tossed his shirt on to the bed and began to unfasten the belt of his trousers. 'Besides, don't forget I was born in Yorkshire. I don't pay good brass for a bed to sleep on't bloody sofa.' It was an uncannily accurate imitation of Grantham at his most obstreperous, and the fact that she knew an overwhelming urge to burst out laughing made her angrier still.

Her voice shaking, she said, 'Then will you ring reception and arrange another room for me?'

Eliot said succinctly, and very definitely, 'No.'

Natalie sent him a look of furious outrage, then swept past him, head held high. The blankets felt itchy without the saving grace of a sheet, and the chaise-longue was just as hard as he'd predicted, she discovered after a very few moments. She wanted to turn over and seek a cosier position, but the light was still on, and the last thing she wanted was to catch any further glimpse of Eliot undressing.

At last there was a click, and the room was plunged into a darkness relieved by the remaining glow from the fire.

His voice reached her mockingly. 'Goodnight, darling. Sleep well.'

As if there was any likelihood of that! Natalie thought, grinding her teeth.

It seemed hours before she finally dropped into an uncomfortable doze, a situation exacerbated by Eliot's soft and even breathing from the bed.

And when she woke, cramped and miserable, the next morning, she was alone. She sat up, grimacing, and sending an apprehensive look towards the bathroom, but there was no sound of water splashing. The fire had been revived and was crackling merrily, she saw, and the curtains were drawn back, revealing that there had been a sharp frost during the night.

Natalie draped her arms morosely round her drawn-up knees and tried to consider what to do next. She could stay where she was, but there seemed little point in that. Besides, she was starving, having eaten so little the night before.

She got up, wincing, and rubbing various tender points on her body. God, but he had a lot to answer for! she thought, seething.

Eliot was seated at a table in the dining room window, eating toast and marmalade, and glancing at the *Times* crossword.

'Ah, here she is now,' he said to the elderly waitress, placing a fresh pot of coffee in front of him. He rose courteously to his feet as Natalie approached. 'You were sleeping so peacefully, darling, I didn't have the heart to disturb you,' he said solemnly, the hazel eyes dancing wickedly.

She took the seat opposite, glaring at him.

'My wife will have bacon, eggs and all the trimmings,' he told the waitress, adding confidentially, 'She's eating for two, you know.'

The woman gave Natalie a motherly smile. 'Well, there's a thing! And I thought you were newlyweds.' She patted Natalie's rigid shoulder. 'We'll feed you up.'

She bustled off, and Natalie stared at her husband. She said shakily, 'Have you no shame at all?'

'Not a great deal,' he admitted, re-folding his paper. 'Have you any plans for today, darling, or would you like to join me on a tour of the local beauty spots? No?

Well, alternatively, why don't we find a lonely piece of fell and spend a few hours shouting and screaming at each other?'

'I don't understand . . .' she began.

'It's quite simple. We need to do something to reduce the tension between us, and a slanging match might be a way of airing our resentments and misgivings about each other. But I can see you don't fancy that idea either.' He pushed back his chair and stood up. 'So, it's your turn to think of something, my reluctant wife, because I'm damned if any son or daughter of mine is going to be born into a situation where their mother flinches every time their father comes near her.' His voice was quiet, but icily, deadly serious. 'I may be back for dinner, I may not. You can let me know what you've decided when I do return.'

It was the longest day Natalie had ever spent, she thought. She walked down to the village and bought some postcards. She strolled part of the way round the lake. She read some of the magazines the hotel provided in the lounge, but she could concentrate on nothing.

Eliot's bitter words seemed to have burned their way into her brain, so that she could think of little else. And no matter what mental arguments she tried to marshal, she was only able to draw one conclusion: having agreed to marry him, albeit unwillingly, she had to try and make the marriage work.

It was almost a relief when he failed to put in an appearance at dinner. Natalie ate grilled trout and drank Perrier water. No alcohol could be allowed to cloud the issue tonight.

When she'd finished her coffee, she went out into the foyer.

'My husband's visiting friends,' she told the recep-
tionist. 'When he returns, will you tell him I've gone up
to bed, please?'

She was assured the message would be relayed, and
went up to the bedroom. She bathed, and scented herself,
putting on her nightgown, before switching off the lamps
and climbing into bed, where she lay quietly, watching
the firelight flickering on the walls.

If peace was going to be declared, there could be no
better setting for it, she thought with a little sigh.

Eliot returned about an hour later. Natalie had been
dozing lightly, but she woke instantly as the door opened,
and lay tense and tingling as he moved quietly round the
room. She was aware of him using the bathroom, of the
rustle of his clothes as he removed them, and the shift
of the mattress as he came to lie beside her.

Suddenly that night when he had driven her slowly
and wildly insane in his arms seemed light years away,
if it had ever happened at all. Far more real were the
nights of painful, nerve-wrenching submission to Tony.

Trembling, she thought despairingly, Oh, don't let it
be like that again. I couldn't bear it . . .

His hand touched the curve of her shoulder, absorbed
the rigidity and the trembling, and was instantly
withdrawn.

He gave a brief, harsh sigh, and turned away from
her. His voice was bitter as it reached her. 'Stop shaking,
Natalie, and get some sleep.'

She turned towards him, her hands seeking him blindly
across the expanse of bed which separated them. 'Eliot—
I . . .'

'No,' he said. 'No, Natalie. You've made your point. Now I'll make mine. This time I want you to leave me alone.'

His back was turned uncompromisingly towards her. She lay staring into the darkness, stunned, bewildered, and lonelier than she'd ever been in her life.

CHAPTER NINE

THEY drove back to Wintersgarth early the following day. At breakfast, Eliot said bitingly, 'I see no point in extending our stay here, do you?'

Natalie shook her head, looking wretchedly down at her plate.

There was a car parked in the yard as Eliot drove under the arch and stopped near the garages, a Rolls-Royce with a chauffeur seated in the front.

'We have visitors, it seems,' Eliot said laconically, switching off the engine. 'Was anyone expected today?'

'No.' Natalie tried to visualise the diary. Sunday was the day most of their owners made the trip to the stables to see their high-bred darlings. Terence Strang came more often, but he invariably drove himself.

'Well, no doubt Grantham is dealing with them.' Eliot lifted the cases out of the back and carried them up to the flat, Natalie following.

He put the baggage down in the bedroom and looked at her. He said, 'I'll use the room next to the bathroom—there's a single bed in there. I'm sure I can count on you to make it up for me. You've had so much practice, after all.'

Colour burned along her cheekbones. She said, 'Eliot, listen to me, please...'

'I should have listened to you before,' he said curtly, cutting across her faltering words. 'The message was coming over loud and clear, but I chose to ignore it.' His mouth twisted. 'To think I accused you of being self-centred! I had no right to coerce you into this marriage, or this baby. But I was arrogant enough—obsessed enough...' He made an impatient gesture. 'Oh, what the hell does it matter? The point is we've made a mistake, but it needn't ruin both our lives. I'd prefer you to live under my roof until the child is born, but after that we can—rethink the situation.'

Natalie hugged her arms across her body. The flat was warm, but she had never felt colder in her life. Tony's rejection of her had been painful, but this was agony, every word a laceration.

She tried to say something, to drag some words together from the wound in her mind, but they wouldn't come. Nothing—nothing made any sense.

Then from the foot of the stairs, Wes's voice shouted, 'Are you there, boss?'

Eliot swung round and went out of the bedroom. 'Yes, what is it? Is something wrong?'

There was a grin in Wes's tone. 'I'd say that depends how you look at it. There's a lady here—Miss Oriel Prince, the actress. She's come to see her horses, seemingly, but she keeps asking for you. Mr Grantham's taken her up to the house for a drink, to get her out of the way. There's been no work done since she got here— those daft devils have been standing round gob-struck!'

Eliot said something sharp and violent under his breath. 'All right, I'll come now,' he called. He looked back at Natalie. 'I thought she was due in two days' time—or did you get the message wrong?'

Natalie straightened her shoulders, stung at the rebuke in his voice. 'No, I didn't,' she returned crisply. 'The arrangement was made by someone else on Miss Prince's behalf. The liaison must have gone wrong at that end.'

He made an impatient sound and plunged off downstairs, leaving Natalie alone in the golden room.

Slowly she unpacked and put her things away, then changed into cord jeans and a sweater. She supposed she had better go down to the office, where Beattie had been nobly holding the fort during her absence, but she lingered, wandering round the flat, at once so familiar and so strange, and trying to imagine what it would be like living there with Eliot, but apart from him in any real sense.

To all intents and purposes she'd been let off the hook—so why wasn't she rejoicing? All she could think of was that when Eliot had turned away from her the previous night, it was as if all the warmth and safety the world held had abandoned her too.

She shook her head in self-derision. I'm crazy, she thought. It's my hormones in uproar because of the baby, that's all.

She was still sitting staring into space half an hour later, when she heard footsteps and voices coming up the stairs. A woman's laughter, she thought in disbelief, staring down in dismay at the elderly jeans.

Oriel Prince came into the room on a gust of perfume. She was of medium height, but the upswept black hair and the delicate spiky heels she wore made her seem taller. She was wrapped in furs which even Natalie's inexperienced eye could see were sables. Her skin was flawless like porcelain, her violet eyes were dark-fringed and luminous, and her smile was radiant, although some of the radiance dimmed a little when she saw Natalie.

She stopped, and said, 'Oh,' and it was a question for Eliot who came into the room behind her.

He said quietly, 'Oriel, I don't think you've met my wife, Natalie.'

'Your wife?' Oriel Prince repeated the words as if they'd been said in some alien language. 'But, Eliot darling, no one told me you were married!'

'It happened only recently.'

'Then you should have invited me to the wedding,' the actress said reproachfully.

'It was a very quiet affair.'

'Yes.' There was a multitude of meanings in that simple monosyllable. Oriel Prince smiled brilliantly. 'Well, I wondered what charm the provinces could possibly have for you, darling, and now I know. She's a sweet child, and we're going to be great friends, I'm sure of it.'

And pigs will grow wings and fly, Natalie thought detachedly.

She said, 'Would you like some coffee, Miss Prince?'

'I'd adore some.' Oriel Prince shrugged off the sables to reveal a woollen sheath dress the same colour as her eyes, clinging to every curve and contour of a perfect figure. 'And call me Oriel, won't you? Your husband and I are such very old friends, after all.'

She might as well have said 'lovers', Natalie thought. The implication was there, direct and unadorned in the casual words. A barb to pierce her, to tear and rend her to the heart, and aimed with deliberate malice. Clearly, the romance with the Arab dignitary was at an end, and the beautiful Oriel had expected to find Eliot single and available.

She said politely, 'I'll go and see about that coffee.'

The first thing she would have to do was find it, she thought, giving a despairing look round the immaculate kitchen. She began opening cupboards at random, her mind elsewhere, whirling, seething.

She found some coffee, and a filter machine, but no sign of any filter papers. She hunted around while the kettle boiled, then realised with a sigh that she would have to ask Eliot where they were. She'd hoped to avoid that. She didn't want Oriel Prince to know how much a stranger she was in her environment.

She went down the passage to the sitting-room. The door was standing ajar, and she pushed it open, in time to hear Oriel Prince say breathily, 'Eliot, you fool!'

Paralysed, Natalie watched as she moved forward into his arms, watched the sinuous curve of her body as she pressed against him in blatant invitation, saw her arms go round his neck and draw him down to her kiss.

She took a step backwards, then another, her fist pressed against her mouth. Then she turned and went swiftly and silently back to the kitchen, and sank down on to one of the chairs.

From a distance, she could hear someone moaning softly, and realised with a shock that it was herself. Pain seized her, lashed her, tore at her. It was impossible to hurt so much and remain whole—remain sane.

She thought, The baby. I'm losing the baby. And it's all I have of him.

There was nausea, hot and bitter in her throat, and she fought it. Fought the clenched fist in the pit of her stomach, and the searing, scalding tears.

With a jerk, the world steadied. The inner agony receded to a manageable distance, making her aware that it wasn't physical in origin, letting her see it for what it shamefully was—jealousy.

She looked blankly across the room.

'All this time,' she whispered silently. 'All this time, I've been falling in love with him, and I never realised—

not until this moment. I had to see him with another woman to know...'

She shook her head in bewilderment and disbelief. It couldn't be true, she tried to argue with herself. Eliot was the outsider, who had turned her world upside down. She had resented him from the moment he had arrived at Wintersgarth. Apart from that one incredible, disastrous night, she'd fought him unceasingly.

Or had she really been fighting herself?

She'd told herself so many times that she hated him, loathed his devastating authority with the horses which even her own father had never matched, disliked the teasing mockery with which he'd answered her overt resentment, was revolted by the physical attraction towards her he had made no attempt to disguise.

And yet, at the same time, she'd never felt more stimulated—more alive. Her reaction to the incident with Michelle Laidlaw should have warned her to examine her motives, her emotions more closely. Instead, she had ignored the danger signals and thrown herself recklessly into his arms.

No, she thought, chewing at her thumbnail, it hadn't been the champagne. It had been the sheer passionate, overwhelming need to touch and be touched, know and be known by the man she loved.

A man who had never shown her more than a transient desire. Who had married her solely to protect his unborn child.

She got up wearily, put cups and saucers on a tray, with cream and sugar, and made coffee from a jar of instant granules.

There was no danger of them not hearing her coming this time, she thought, as she carried the rattling tray along the passage. She almost knocked at the door before entering—but not quite.

Oriel was sitting on one of the sofas, legs elegantly and revealingly crossed, while Eliot was standing in front of the newly lit fire, one arm resting lightly on the mantelpiece. The atmosphere, Natalie thought tautly, could well be described as—loaded.

She put the tray down. 'Sorry for the delay.' She looked at Eliot. 'We seem to have run out of filter papers, darling.'

'Oh, it really doesn't matter,' Oriel broke in sweetly. 'I'm sure it will be delicious anyway. And Eliot and I haven't noticed the passage of time at all—we had so much to catch up on.'

Natalie wondered what would happen if she took the entire tray and upended its contents in Miss Prince's violet lap. Her pulses throbbed with the effort to appear calm, and unsuspecting.

Oriel turned the dazzle of her smile towards Eliot. 'I suppose I'll have to forgive you, darling, for bringing my sweethearts to this backwater. They seem to be in excellent condition. That rather surly girl who sees to them seems to know her job.'

'She's an excellent worker in every way,' Natalie said briefly. And a shrewd judge of character, she added silently.

Oriel bestowed a vague look at her, as if surprised to hear her speak, and switched her attention back to Eliot, her voice intimately lowered. 'I had a stopover in Rome, to do some shopping, and I dined with the Contessa. She said to tell you that colt Genista is turning out just as you said—and why didn't you go and work for her, if you wanted to train horses.' She turned to Natalie. 'Your clever husband could have chosen any stables in

Europe, I do believe. And he winds up here, working for that extraordinary man! Very worthy, I suppose, but a rough diamond to say the least.'

Eliot said drily, 'The rough diamond you mention happens to be Natalie's father.'

'Oh!' Oriel clapped her hands to her mouth in a pretty show of penitence. 'My dear, how incredibly tactless of me! Now, how can I make it up to you? I know. Both of you must—simply must have dinner with me tonight at my hotel.' She shrugged. 'I can't vouch for the food, of course, but we'll just have to pray it's edible.'

Natalie set down her cup, not looking at Eliot. Let him make some excuse, she begged silently, let him refuse. Oh, please...

After a pause, he said, 'That's kind of you, Oriel. We'd like to accept, wouldn't we, darling?'

She was saved from having to reply by the insistent burble of the telephone. She excused herself, and hurried to answer. It was Beattie.

'Well, you're a pair of sly-boots, creeping back like this,' she scolded. 'Not that we're not grateful, you understand. Have you met that appalling woman?'

'Yes.' Natalie's taut mouth relaxed into a reluctant smile. 'Oh, Beattie, you're wonderful! You do cheer me up.'

'A bride on her honeymoon shouldn't need cheering up,' chided Beattie. 'But acting on the twin premise that the cupboards in that wonderful kitchen of yours are probably bare, and no one can live on love alone, in spite of what they say, I thought you might like to have dinner with us tonight?'

'Oh, I'd have loved to.' Natalie could have wept. 'But you're just five minutes too late. We—we've got another invitation.'

'Not to worry,' Beattie said cheerfully. 'We'll arrange another time. And your father will be down to see you as soon as the coast is clear.' She giggled. 'I'm afraid the glamorous Miss Prince isn't his kind of owner at all. He says that scent she uses has started up his sinus trouble!'

Natalie's grin widened involuntarily. 'Well, for once Dad and I are in complete agreement,' she said, and rang off.

Back in the sitting room, Oriel was preparing to take her leave, sliding her arms into the sable coat which Eliot held for her, staying close to him just a few seconds too long.

She tapped Natalie's cheek with a careless finger as she went past her to the door. '*Au revoir*, my dear. It's been delightful meeting you. Eliot's a very lucky man.'

Eliot accompanied her to her car. Natalie carried the tray of dirty cups back to the kitchen, and ran hot water into the sink, while she tried to think what to do next. Did Eliot have so poor an opinion of her mentality as to assume she didn't know what was going on? she wondered bitterly. Because that hurt almost as much as the jealousy.

By the time he came back to the kitchen she was almost at shouting and screaming point, ready to throw each and every one of the carefully washed dishes at his head, only to discover, as she turned to face him, that Grantham was looming behind him in the doorway.

'So you're back.' His embarrassed hug was accompanied by a searching look. 'You look pale.'

'I feel fine.' She kept her voice light and non-committal. 'How about you?'

'I saw the doctor yesterday. He seems satisfied.' Grantham pursed his lips. 'Though after what I've been through in the past couple of days, it's a wonder I'm not back in intensive care. That bloody Midstream tipped young Micky off, bad-tempered devil, and took off like a bat out of hell. We caught him on the main road— the damned main road, would you believe!' He shook his head in a mixture of disbelief and admiration. 'By rights, he should have broken his cranky neck. But he can't half jump.'

'How's Micky?' asked Natalie.

Her father snorted. 'Broken collarbone, and serves him right. Just sheer lack of concentration. Claims something shone in his eyes.'

Eliot's brows lifted. 'Did anyone else notice anything?'

'Of course not. There was nowt to notice,' her father retorted testily. 'It's never their own bad riding with these lads when they get thrown.'

Eliot said slowly, 'Micky isn't usually a bad rider.' He paused. 'And it's bad news that he's going to be out of action for a while. We're going to be damned short-handed.'

'Well, there we did have a bit of luck,' Grantham said with satisfaction. 'This other lad turned up yesterday— said he'd heard we were expanding and wondered whether there might be a vacancy.'

Natalie stared at him. 'But we never take on casuals like that,' she objected.

'He's not some fly-by-night,' said Grantham impatiently. 'He's been working up in a small stable in Northumberland, but the trainer's retiring at the end of the season. He's got his cards and his references all right and tight. They're in the office, waiting for you.' He exchanged a look with Eliot. 'And while we're on the subject, you may as well know I'm advertising for another secretary.'

'But why?'

'Because Eliot and I think you should start to take things easy,' he said flatly. 'You're too thin, for one thing.'

'I'm as strong as a horse!' Natalie protested furiously.

Grantham was unmoved. 'And a lot of funny things can happen to mares when they're foaling, as you should know, my girl. So you're going to be wrapped in cotton wool. You're going to rest more—and eat more too. I want my grandson to be born strong and healthy.'

Eliot's tone was mild, but there was an unholy gleam of amusement in his eyes as he looked at his father-in-law. 'Has it occurred to you that this—er—colt you're expecting could turn out to be a little filly?'

At any other time, the look of dismay on Grantham's face would have appealed to Natalie's sense of the ridiculous too, but she was feeling too bruised for laughter.

She said tautly, 'Would you please stop talking about me as if I was a brood animal! And I'm not impressed by all this—talk of tender loving care. You don't want me involved in the stables in any way—not even marginally—either of you!'

Her voice rose hysterically, and Eliot's face sobered immediately.

He said, 'Natalie, that isn't true. The work you do is invaluable, and I know you're capable of more. No one's trying to shut you out, believe me. When the baby's born . . .'

'Oh, yes,' she said bitterly. 'The scrap of humanity around whom the universe revolves. The excuse to shuffle me off to the sidelines. Well, I'm beginning to hate this baby—almost as much as I hate both of you!'

She burst into tears and ran out of the room, ignoring her father's outraged bellow, 'Natalie!'

She flew into the bedroom, slamming the door behind her for good measure, before flinging herself across the bed. She wept until all the tension, wretchedness and misery of the past weeks seemed to have been purged out of her. Somewhere amid the storm of tears, she thought she heard Grantham leaving, but she couldn't be sure.

The door didn't open for another half-hour, however. Eliot came in carrying a cup and saucer which he placed beside the bed.

'I've brought you some tea,' he said.

Natalie struggled to a sitting position, scrubbing her wet cheeks defensively with a handkerchief. 'I'm not an invalid.'

'No,' he said grimly. 'A pain in the neck would be a more apt description just at the moment.'

She might have expunged some of the bitterness, but her temper still remained. She gasped, and her hand swung back, aiming to make contact with his unsmiling face, but before the blow could reach its target, his fingers had closed implacably round her wrist.

His voice was like steel. 'Forget it, Natalie. You don't hit me now, or at any future time, because I can't retaliate—much as I might like to,' he added icily.

He released her almost contemptuously, and said, 'About your little outburst just now, I've already come to terms with the fact that I've ruined your life. So say what you like to me—although I'd prefer you to reserve your strictures for when we're alone together. But leave your father out of it. He has nothing but your well-being at heart, and he doesn't deserve to be hated for that.' He paused. 'Now, wash you face and drink your tea. You're going to dinner tonight, not a funeral.'

Natalie said, 'I'm not going anywhere tonight. I'm staying here.'

His brows snapped together. 'What the hell are you talking about?'

She said coldly, 'I'm not a complete fool. I know quite well tonight's invitation doesn't really include me. It was only extended—for form's sake. Well, I haven't the slightest wish to intrude on your reunion with your— lady-friend.'

Eliot said sharply, 'You don't know what you're talking about. Of course you're coming with me.'

Natalie shook her head. 'No, I'm not. It's you she wants—your unencumbered presence. Well, go to her.'

He sat down wearily on the edge of the bed. 'Natalie, I never pretended you were the first woman in my life. But, for God's sake, this is history you're talking about. That—episode was over a long time ago.'

'Well, Miss Prince doesn't seem to think so. She was practically eating you with her eyes this afternoon!'

'She probably did the same to Grantham,' he said drily. 'And to Wes—and every other lad in the yard. It's part of her stock in trade—as natural to her as breathing.'

She said breathlessly, 'But I bet she didn't kiss Grantham—or any of the others. Or are you trying to tell me that's part of her stock in trade too?'

Eliot was very still. 'No, I'm not trying to tell you that.'

'Good.' She was shaking inside. 'So now you know why I don't believe your protests, Eliot—and why I won't be joining you. I'd only be in the way. At least . . .' She stopped abruptly.

'At least—what?' His voice bit.

At least Tony never made me meet any of his mistresses, let alone have dinner with them, had been the unspoken words which had leapt so betrayingly to mind.

She said drearily, 'It doesn't matter.'

'No,' he said, too quietly. 'You could be right.'

He got up and went out of the room, slamming the door behind him. Natalie sank back against her pillows. The inner trembling was spreading through her entire body now. She hadn't meant to say all that. She'd meant to be very calm, very controlled. To invent some minor ailment, a headache, more nausea, a pain in her back—something to keep her at home.

Something, too, which might have kept him at her side, she confessed to herself. She was beginning to realise how and why some women used vague ill-health as a weapon to hold over their husbands' heads. One hint that she wasn't feeling well would have been enough to arouse his concern, even if that concern was for his child rather than herself, she thought, wincing.

She began to drink some of her tea, grateful for its consoling warmth.

It was beginning to occur to her that she might have played straight into Oriel Prince's hands. That the actress's invitation to her, her whole attitude, might have been intended to provoke this very reaction in her. She groaned. Hadn't she learned anything from those bitter years with Tony?

She shook her head. By the time she'd realised what was going on, their marriage had been virtually over anyway.

She bit her lip. She hadn't fought for Tony because she hadn't wanted him. That last appalling, fatal row had been sparked off by hurt pride rather than any deeper emotion. She'd come to terms with that in guilt and regret a long time ago. If she'd let him go he would probably be alive now, and married to the woman he was leaving her for.

Yet within a few hours of realising she loved Eliot, she was passively surrendering him to another woman, instead of fighting for him.

I should be going with him, she thought, sitting bolt upright. I should be playing her game—using the body language, sitting close to him, fluttering my eyelashes, touching him all the time—letting her know that I'm the lady with his ring on her finger.

And at the same time I'd be telling Eliot, without words, that I love him and want him.

Faint colour rose in her face as she contemplated what that would lead to. Perhaps tomorrow she would wake in his arms in this golden room. And she would see to it thereafter that they were never parted again, she told herself vehemently. She would be all the wife, all the woman Eliot would ever want.

Starting now. She scrambled off the bed and dashed to the wardrobe, rooting through it until she found what she was looking for.

It was a simple floor-length gown in emerald green silk, with heavy gold embroidery round the deeply slashed neckline. Like the velvet lounging suit, it had been another impulse buy which she'd instantly regretted, but now the dress seemed to have endless possibilities. She grabbed her dressing gown and the minimum underwear the dress required and went to the bathroom. A damp towel on the floor and a tang of cologne in the air revealed that Eliot had been there before her. She listened, but could hear no sound from the room next door. She ran a bath swiftly, and washed with equal speed, splashing cold water on her face to remove any lingering marks of tears. Tonight, she thought, she was going to look radiant if it killed her!

She rehearsed silently what she would say when Eliot came to say goodbye to her, and ask her to change her mind, as she knew he would. She would keep it simple and down to earth, she thought, so that there would be no more misunderstandings.

Back in the bedroom, she made up her face with care, accentuating the colour and shape of her green eyes with shadow and liner, and painting a clear bright coral on to her lips. She slid the dress over her head and brushed out her hair on her shoulders, then stared at herself. She looked exotic, she thought with satisfaction, and distinctly provocative.

Then she sat down and waited. The minutes dragged past, and she began to glance restively at her watch. Where was Eliot? They would have to be leaving very soon.

She waited a while longer, then went along to the room he was using, and knocked on the door. There was no answer, and after a moment, she turned the handle and looked in. The room was empty, the clothes he had been wearing earlier lying across the still unmade-up bed.

Natalie turned, and almost run down to the sitting-room. It was empty too, the fire banked up behind a spark guard. She swallowed. The flat was quiet—too quiet. All she could hear, apart from the faint crackling of the logs, was the sound of her own rapid breathing.

She went slowly to the window and looked down through the gathering darkness at the place where the Porsche had been standing since their return. But she already knew it would not be there.

Eliot hadn't come to say goodbye, or to persuade her to go with him. He had taken her quite cynically at her word, she realised dazedly, and gone to meet Oriel Prince, leaving her here alone, and more frightened than she'd ever been in her life.

CHAPTER TEN

SHE STAYED where she was, staring sightlessly out of the window for a long time, the she quietly turned and went back to the golden bedroom, and took off the beautiful dress, replacing it with the jeans and sweater she had been wearing earlier. She went into the kitchen and took an apple from the bowl of fruit in the centre of the table, cutting it into quarters before going downstairs.

Evening stables was over, and the horses settled for the night, as she slipped into the second yard and made her way to Jasmine's box. She saw the mare's head turn as she approached, and the elegant ears lift as her name was called.

Natalie fed her the apple, and laid her cheek against the soft muzzle. Sharon exercised Jasmine for her now, as Grantham had given strict instructions that she wasn't to ride any more while she was pregnant. She'd been disposed to argue, but had thought better of it, reminding herself that her mother's early and tragic death must be colouring his thinking, although he never talked about it openly.

'I miss you,' she whispered. Horses were such uncomplicated beasts. They didn't hurt you, or betray you—unless they were spoiled, imperious and bad-tempered like Midstream, that was. But he was a law unto himself, as befitted a future champion. Because that was what he undoubtedly would be. Already his progress was being followed in the racing columns, and predictions were being made which Grantham raged over, and Eliot shrugged away in displeasure.

Natalie stayed talking to Jasmine for a few more minutes, petting her and rubbing her neck, then she turned away with a sigh, jumping visibly as a shadow detached itself from the surrounding shadows and came towards her. It was no one she'd seen before.

'Who are you?' As she stared at him, she had the odd feeling she'd seen him before.

'Roland Bakewell, miss. I only arrived yesterday. Hope I didn't startle you.'

'Well, you did,' she said rather shortly. 'What are you doing?'

'I left my jacket in the tack room—got all the way back to the digs before I realised. Really mild it is tonight.'

'Yes.' Natalie went on staring at him. She said, 'Haven't we met before?'

'Oh, no, miss. I'd have remembered.' He gave her a pleasant smile. 'But they say everyone has a double, don't they?'

She shrugged. 'I suppose so. Well, goodnight, Roland. Or is it Roly?'

'That's what the other lads call me, miss.'

'Then I will too. Now get back to your digs, or you'll be late for supper.' She watched him disappear, then turned back towards the flat with another sigh. Her mind must be playing her tricks, and small wonder.

She was half tempted to go up to the house for company, but Beattie would want to know what had happened to the dinner invitation she'd mentioned, and she didn't feel equal to inventing a plausible explanation. And her stepmother clearly thought the marriage was going to be a great success. She wouldn't want to hear it was on the rocks already.

There was some cheese in the refrigerator, and she made herself a sandwich, and washed it down with a glass of milk. She wandered back into the sitting room and turned on the hi-fi. There was a tape of Eliot's in the machine already, and the sound of Roberta Flack singing 'The first time ever I saw your face' filled the room. Wincing, Natalie switched it off. She didn't need reminding of the first time she'd seen Eliot, or kissed him, or lain with him. She found some nice safe Debussy instead.

And when she'd had as much music and as much loneliness as she could stand, she went to bed.

She heard the case clock in the passage chime midnight before she finally fell asleep, only to wake with a start a couple of hours later. She sat up, wondering what had disturbed her, and saw a crack of light under the door. And yet she had switched all the lights off before coming to bed. So Eliot had not spent the whole night with his lady.

She pushed back the covers and got out of bed, treading softly over to the door, and listening. She thought she could hear music very faintly in the distance, and after a brief hesitation she opened the door and walked, barefoot, down the passage to the sitting-room.

The door was closed, but the music was stronger now. She pushed opened the door and walked in. Eliot was sprawled on one of the sofas, his long legs stretched out in front of him, jacket off and tie loosened, his eyes closed, and his hand clamped round a tumbler containing a generous measure of whisky. The decanter, Natalie saw, was on the floor at his feet.

She didn't think she'd made any sound, but his eyes opened, focusing on her as if he was having difficulty in remembering who she was.

She said inanely, 'You're back.'

'So it would seem.' He frowned. 'What is it? Why did you wake up? Did I have the music on too loud? Or are you not feeling well?'

'I'm all right.' She sat on the sofa opposite, tucking her bare feet under the hem of her sprigged Victorian-style nightdress.

'Did you have a pleasant evening?' As soon as she'd asked the stupid question, she could have bitten her tongue out.

'How kind of you to enquire,' he said too cour-teously. 'I had——' the pause was deliberate, she knew, 'a fantastic time. Shall I go into details for you?'

'No,' she said tautly.

There was a silence. Eliot watched her, a cynical smile playing round his mouth. 'How sweet you look tonight, my dear wife.' He drank some of his whisky. 'Like some innocent schoolgirl—a little virgin, untouched by human hand. Except that you're not a virgin, are you, darling? You've been married before to a man called Tony Drummond, and now you're married, for want of a better word, to me. So why, when I look at you, do I get "virgin" in word association?' He thought for a moment, then nodded. 'I remember—it's because you can't stand my touching you, or coming anywhere near you.'

Natalie said in a low voice, 'Eliot, please.'

'Eliot does not damned well please,' he said with swift bitterness. 'If you don't like the conversation, Natalie, you can always go back to bed. I've had a surfeit of female company this evening already.'

Now, she knew, was not the time, but if she remained silent she might lose her courage altogether. And the words she had rehearsed earlier that evening were there, begging to be spoken.

She said, 'Eliot, I came to say I was sorry—about the honeymoon—and——' she swallowed, 'and everything that's happened since.'

There was a pause. Then, 'Your gracious apology is equally graciously accepted, darling,' he said. 'But if you're waiting for me to grovel in return, you'll wait a hell of a long time.'

'No, I didn't intend that. I—I shouldn't have behaved as I did, said the things I said. I—I blame myself...'

'Well, you can stop grovelling too,' he said brusquely. 'It's neither pretty nor necessary.'

'But I need to make you understand.' She looked down at her hands, locked together in her lap. 'In spite of everything, can't we begin again—make a fresh start?'

There was an even longer pause. 'Now, why should we want to do that?' he asked politely.

Because I love you.

She looked at him, at the mockery on the dark face, and swallowed back the words, twisting a fold of nightgown between nervous fingers.

She said, 'For the baby's sake—maybe we should try...'

'Ah, for the baby.' Eliot reached for the decanter, liberally topping up his glass. 'That, of course, makes all the difference.' He drank some of the whisky, staring down into the glass. Then he said quietly, 'Go to bed, Natalie. We'll talk some other time.'

'Why not now?' She bit her lip.

He looked at her derisively. 'Because, my darling, I am in the process of getting drunk—not a condition that lends itself to serious conversation. So, on your way, sweetheart, there's a good girl.'

She said quietly, 'Don't treat me like a child.'

'Why not?' he jeered. 'It's altogether safer than treating you like a woman, as we both know to our cost.'

Uncertainly, Natalie got to her feet. She said shakily, 'Are you planning to ride out to exercise tomorrow?'

'Naturally. I never allow a mere hangover to get in the way of my duties.'

'But you won't ride Midstream—will you?'

'I certainly will.' He sent her a cordial smile. 'It will be interesting to see which of us is in the bloodiest mood.'

'That's madness!' she protested. 'You'll be in no fit state to ride him. You have to have all your wits about you—you've said so yourself.'

He shrugged. 'Then call this a change of tactics. Besides,' he swallowed some more whisky, 'I might even fall off and break my neck, which would be the solution to all sorts of problems. You could revert to being a widow—all the status of marriage, without any of the more distasteful obligations. And my money as as bonus. It should suit you very well.'

Natalie said quietly, 'If that's what you think, there's no more to be said.' She walked to the door, stumbling a little over the hem of the nightdress.

Back in the bedroom, she closed the door and leaned against it for a moment, trying to regulate her breathing. What a fool she'd been to think that a single, simplistic approach could solve all the problems between them. What a crass, naïve idiot!

She undid the small pearl buttons at her throat and walked over to the window, opening the casement and taking deep, grateful gulps of the cold air which streamed in.

She'd spent a lot of nights at this window in earlier days, sitting out Tony's increasingly delayed returns from race meetings. She'd experienced bewilderment, shock, hurt, and finally anger as their marriage had deteriorated into bitter recrimination.

'You don't think I married you because I fell madly in love with you?' Tony had asked derisively that last evening, as he threw a change of clothing into an overnight bag. 'I quite fancied you at first, but I married you for a stake in Wintersgarth. But the game isn't worth the candle any more. I'm not hanging round here, getting frozen to death in bed each night, just so that I can step into a dead man's shoes some time in the unforeseeable future. Jan's divorce settlement is big enough to keep us in comfort for a very long time. She's thinking of buying a pub, anyway, and she'll need me to help her run it eventually.'

She had looked at him with contempt, seeing with merciless clarity the weakness and self-satisfaction that underlay the surface good looks.

She'd said, 'You're lucky, Tony, finding another wealthy idiot to lap up your little-boy charm. But it's beginning to wear very thin, so don't count on it happening a third time when Jan throws you out.'

'You're not throwing me out.' He'd been shaking with rage as he zipped up the case, cursing obscenely because something was caught in the fastening. 'I was leaving you anyway. You think I'd live any longer with you, you . . .' He'd stormed on and on at her, heaping insult on insult, while she'd faced him, outwardly calm, but inwardly cringing.

When he finally left, closing the door behind him with a slam which made the whole flat reverberate, Natalie had sunk down on the floor because her legs wouldn't support her.

Tony, her husband, had finally left, and although she had told him to go, she should have been devastated. Instead she had felt an appalling sense of relief—and found herself wondering if the unknown Jan would be as delighted to have him moving in with her as he had so confidently averred.

But that was something none of them would ever know. Tony's driving, like his riding, had always verged on the reckless, and that night he had taken one chance too many, his car ploughing into the side of a goods train on an unmanned crossing.

Her father had grieved for Tony, and she had allowed him to do so, keeping the truth about his flagrant infidelities a close secret. She told herself she had to be partly to blame for the failure of their relationship. She should have recognised her initial feeling for him for what it was—a brief, soon-to-be-burned-out infatuation. But once married, she should have made more effort to make the marriage work, especially its intimate side. Her abysmal failure in this direction made her believe that Tony could have been right—that maybe she was incomplete in some way, incapable of being a real woman.

What she hadn't bargained for was Eliot—the outsider—coming into her life. Or for that one wild, passionate night which had taught her the devastating truth about herself and her own sensuality.

She sighed, leaning her forehead against the cool glass, relishing the stillness of the night. And the next morning she'd panicked and run from him, like a frightened animal seeking sanctuary.

She stiffened suddenly, frowning because the silence outside was being disturbed. There was something alien in the pattern of the night, something that should not have been there. Somewhere—diminishing into the distance—the unmistakable ring of a horse's hooves.

Natalie leaned out of the window, listening feverishly, straining her ears as she tried to gauge distance and direction. Then she ran for the door, almost flinging herself down the passage and into the sitting-room. Eliot was standing by the hearth, looking down into the flames. His head turned abruptly at her tempestuous entry, his eyes widening in incredulity as she ran towards him. The glass went flying, its contents scattering on the carpet as he strode towards her. He caught her by the shoulders, jerking her forward savagely into his arms.

He said harshly, 'I told you to go to bed, Natalie. You shouldn't have come back. You shouldn't be here...' His mouth fastened on hers, urgently, hungrily. His hands scorched through her nightdress, seeking the contours of breast and hip and thigh, as his lips tore from her the response she could not deny him. But as her need for him drove her senses to the brink of fainting, and rose like a sob in her throat, some remnant of sanity still remained.

'Eliot.' She could barely control the words, utter them coherently. 'One of the horses is loose—I heard it!'

He was very still suddenly. He held her away from him, his eyes searching her face.

He said, 'Is—that what you came to say?'

As she bowed her head in silent acquiescence, she heard him sigh, briefly and bitterly. There was a silence, then he said, 'This horse—you're sure you heard it?'

'Ninety-nine per cent sure,' she said huskily. 'I'd opened the bedroom window, you see, and at first I didn't realise what I was hearing.'

Eliot nodded, but she knew he didn't really believe her. Security was always so tight in the yard. At evening stables each night, the fastening of each box was always checked.

He said, 'I'll take a torch and have a look.'

'Shall I phone the police—warn them?'

'Later, if it's necessary.'

Natalie went back to the bedroom and dragged on jeans and a sweater, sliding her arms into a quilted bodywarmer.

When she entered the yard, she could see Eliot's torch moving. She went to join him.

'Anything?'

'Nothing,' he said curtly.

She flushed. 'I wasn't imagining it—I know I wasn't.' She paused. 'Have you looked at the new boxes?'

'I checked them first,' he said impatiently. He walked into the small yard, Natalie following, and swept the torchlight round it. At the end of the block, one of the doors swung open on its hinges.

Eliot swore furiously under his breath. He muttered, 'How the hell . . .'

'Oh God!' Natalie clapped her hands over her mouth. 'It's Jasmine's box. It must be my fault. I came down tonight and gave her some apple, like I always do. I must have leant against the bolt, dislodged it somehow.'

Eliot said grimly, 'I fail to see how, but we'll discuss that later. The thing now is to get the horse back.' He paused. 'Can you drive the Land Rover?' She nodded. 'Go and get the keys from the office, and get the thing out. I'll fetch a halter.' He added more gently. 'She can't have got far. We'll catch her, and I'll walk her back.'

Jasmine wasn't young any more, Natalie thought as she headed the Land Rover down the long private drive that led to the road from the stables. It was unlikely she would have put on a great burst of speed. They'd probably find the horse grazing at the side of the road, she assured herself out of the welter of guilt which assailed her.

But there was no familiar shape moving on the verge, no whinny of recognition.

She said, 'Which way?' and Eliot shrugged.

'We could toss a coin. Let's try left first.'

Natalie drove carefully, peering through the windscreen. After a while she said tautly, 'This is hopeless. We must have gone the wrong way.'

'I'm afraid you're right. We'd better turn round.'

They had driven back, past the entry to the stables, when Natalie saw ahead of her the blaze of headlights cutting the night sky. She said, with a gasp, half to herself, 'Oh, I prayed there wouldn't be any traffic. She's not good in traffic, she never has been.'

Even as she spoke, she heard the distant crash, the breaking glass, the sound of shouting, a girl screaming.

Eliot groaned. He said tersely, 'Drive.'

It was a Ford Sierra. It had slewed across the road and half mounted the bank, narrowly missing a tree. The headlights were broken, and the offside wing was a mess.

Natalie took this in almost involuntarily. She saw the dark shape of the mare lying in the road, making frantic efforts to rise, and pulled in at the side, slamming on the brakes. As she fumbled with the door, Eliot's hand descended on her arm.

He said, 'Stay here, darling. Let me go and look.'

She'd heard that note in her father's voice on more than one occasion, and knew what it meant. With a sob, she dropped her head forward on to the steering wheel.

He wasn't gone long. She looked at him, saw the compassion in his eyes and said weakly, 'It's bad—isn't it?'

Eliot nodded. 'She's broken her leg. And I think she has other injuries.'

Natalie made a little sound in her throat.

He said, 'There's a cottage a bit further down. The crash woke the people there, and one of them's ringing the vet now, and the police.' He paused. 'The couple in the car are very shaken up. They're only young. They were coming back from a party. The girl was driving, so she'd been on orange juice all night. It seems she adores animals and she's nearly hysterical. Her boyfriend can't cope, and neither, frankly, can I. Will you come and talk to her, try and calm her down.'

The girl was sitting on the verge, crying monotonously while her dishevelled young man fussed over her. He let Natalie take his place with evident relief.

The girl took Natalie's hands into a grip that hurt. 'It's your horse, isn't it—your husband said so.' Her voice was choking. 'I couldn't do anything—that's what's so awful. I just couldn't! I hadn't had a drink all night, I wasn't even speeding, and when I came round the corner, there she was in the middle of the road. I—I swerve even for hedgehogs. I tried—I did try...'

Natalie put her arm round the heaving shoulders. 'You could have been killed yourself,' she said gently. 'Just be thankful that you're both all right.'

'But what was she *doing* there?' the girl asked unanswerably. She began to sob again. 'And Daddy's car—what will he say when he sees it?'

A procession of people began to arrive—the vet, the police, and ambulance to take the young couple to the nearest casualty department for a check-up, a breakdown van for the crippled Sierra.

In the middle of it all, Eliot came over to Natalie. 'One of the policemen is going to drive you home,' he said quietly. 'I've explained that I've been drinking, and undoubtedly over the limit.'

She knew what he was trying to spare her, and got to her feet. 'Won't they need statements?'

'Yes, but not this very minute.'

The policeman could not have been kinder. The worst moment came as Natalie climbed down from the Land Rover, and saw the unused halter still waiting in the back. The policeman took one look at her white face and quivering lips and put an arm round her. He said, 'Come indoors, love, and show me where the kitchen is. I'll make you some tea.'

They were on their second mugs when Eliot returned. His face looked haggard under his tan as he came into the kitchen. He came over to Natalie and dropped to one knee beside her chair. He said gently, 'Are you all right?' She nodded wordlessly, and he pressed her fingers swiftly with his. 'Why don't you go to bed for what's left of the night? I'll see the officer out.'

She was too weary, too heartsore to protest. In the bedroom, she found herself shivering uncontrollably as she undressed and put on her nightdress once more. The bed felt vast and chilly, a desert in which she was stranded alone. She lay listening to the sounds of leavetaking, the closing of doors. She heard Eliot's returning footsteps pause outside her door. She said, 'I'm awake.'

He stood by the door and looked at her. 'Can I get you something?' He looked round. 'Do you have any sleeping tablets—tranquillisers?'

'No.' She sat up. 'Eliot, will you tell me about it, please? Did she suffer?'

'No,' he said. 'Derek's a terrific guy. He wouldn't have allowed it.'

'Yes.' There was a silence, then she said, 'I feel so terrible—like a murderess.'

'Don't say that. Don't even think it.' He came and sat down on the edge of the bed, taking her hands in his. 'Natalie, you can't unbolt a door by leaning on it, you know that.'

'But what other answer is there?'

'I wish to God I knew.' He gave her a strained smile. 'Goodnight. Try and get some rest.' He made to stand up, but she clung to him.

'Eliot, don't leave me. Stay with me—please!'

His mouth tightened. He tried to release himself from her clasp. 'You're upset. You don't know what you're saying.'

'I do—I do,' she told him desperately. 'Eliot, do I have to beg you?'

There was a silence. Bitter hazel eyes looked into imploring green ones, and he sighed.

'What do you think I'm made of—stone?' He kicked off his shoes and shed the waterproof jacket he was wearing, before lying down beside her.

Her heart was beating so rapidly it hurt. She said, 'Aren't you going to—undress properly?'

'No,' he said curtly. 'I'm staying, and that's it.'

His arm held her, her head rested on his shoulder, but it was far from the reunion she'd dreamed of.

From now on, Natalie thought, her mind drifting as sleep closed down on her, she would make do with reality.

But when she eventually opened her eyes to the full light of day, much, much later, she found that reality was waking up alone once more.

CHAPTER ELEVEN

'DARLING,' Beattie said. 'You must stop blaming yourself. It can't be good for you, or the baby.'

Natalie sighed. 'I can't help it,' she said quietly. 'I'm almost thankful Dad's taken on a new secretary. It means I don't have to go near the yard—I don't have to see Jasmine's empty box.'

'But you didn't do anything. You weren't responsible. Eliot proved that, surely? He showed you it was impossible for you to have dislodged the bolt in the way you described.'

'Yes,' Natalie said neutrally. 'He's been—very kind about it all.'

And if kindness had been all she wanted from him, she thought detachedly, she would have been happy indeed. As it was . . .

She went on, 'And it's proved something else to me as well. Daddy was right all along when he said I wasn't tough enough for his kind of life. It—it doesn't even seem to matter any more.'

Beattie patted her arm. 'That's because you're having a baby, and that's absorbing all your attention.' She chuckled. 'It'll be different once it's born. You'll be in there slugging, fighting for your rights all over again!'

Natalie thought, *I wonder* . . .

'How did your ante-natal check up go?' asked Beattie.

Natalie shrugged. 'Fine—apparently. I'm in excellent health, and so's the baby, although I don't know how they can tell. I haven't even got a bump yet.'

She flushed slightly as she remembered the doctor's cheerful, 'And it's all right to resume normal marital relations, Mrs Lang, if you haven't already. There can be a slight risk in the early weeks sometimes, but that's behind you now. Be happy. Enjoy your marriage and your pregnancy.'

But that was easier said than done, she thought wretchedly, when Eliot hadn't even crossed the threshold of their bedroom since the night of Jasmine's accident.

He was invariably polite when they did encounter each other—considerate even—but aloof, creating a barrier that she seemed unable to penetrate. And he never touched her, even accidentally. Indeed, he seemed to go out of his way to avoid physical contact with her.

Although she had to acknowledge that he had plenty to occupy his mind these days. A number of owners, including Terence Strang, had been concerned when a brief story about Jasmine's accident had appeared in the papers.

In fact Mr Strang had descended on them like a thunderbolt, demanding to know what kind of set-up allowed valuable horses to roam on main roads in the early hours, and what guarantee there was that it wouldn't happen again.

A number of others had asked the same thing. And Oriel Prince had removed her two, insisting that Sharon go with them. Natalie had been really sorry to see her go, but Sharon had been cheerful enough.

'Going back to Lambourn means I'll be nearer the family,' she said. 'And I knew she wouldn't leave well alone.' She gave Natalie a cryptic glance. 'Not once she found out Mr Lang was married. Sort of—removed her incentive.'

Natalie had smiled dutifully, but she thought, *No, it didn't...*

And there were other problems too—the continuing publicity about Midstream and his potential, for one.

'You can't go up on the gallops these days for pressmen with cameras jumping out of the gorse at you,' Wes said gloomily.

Even Grantham had acceded grudgingly that maybe Micky's fall could be attributed to being dazzled by a camera lens rather than carelessness.

And in a fortnight Midstream was to compete in his first major race since coming to Wintersgarth—the Whitstone Cup, and he was already, because of the newspaper stories, being heavily backed.

As she walked back to the flat, hands tucked into the pockets of her sheepskin coat, Natalie wondered whether Eliot would ask her to go with him to watch Midstream. He had never suggested, since their marriage, that she accompany him racing. It seemed that she was the outsider now.

She'd thought he would be up on the gallops for the second exercise of the day, but when she walked into the kitchen he was sitting at the table.

'Oh.' Natalie halted. 'Did you want to speak to me about something? I'm sorry—I was up at the house with Beattie.'

'Yes, I guessed that. I've just made some coffee. Would you like some?'

She wrinkled her nose. 'Perhaps not. It seems to be the only thing that still makes me feel a little bit sick.' She paused. 'I saw the doctor this morning. He says everything's fine.'

'Good.' His tone was polite without any real warmth.

Natalie bit her lip. 'I'll go and change, and make a start on lunch. We're having goulash today,' she went on, making an effort to speak lightly. 'Beattie's been giving me lessons, you'll be relieved to hear.'

'Will it stretch?' he asked. 'Calum Carmichael's coming down this morning to have a look at Midstream, and I'd like to be able to offer him a meal afterwards.'

'Yes, of course.' He couldn't be more formal, Natalie thought miserably, if she was some newly engaged housekeeper. Except that she'd probably have had her cards by now. She was still no culinary expert, and although Eliot offered no overt criticism, he still often cooked the evening meal himself. 'I'll try not to burn anything,' she joked weakly, but he didn't return her smile.

He picked up an envelope and slid it across the table to her. 'Do you know this house?' he asked.

The envelope contained several typed pages, and a number of photographs in colour. Natalie's eyes widened incredulously as she spotted an estate agent's logo.

'But this is Highbeck House!' she exclaimed. 'Surely Mrs Grosvenor isn't selling?'

'It seems she has to. She's well into her eighties, and she's had a couple of falls lately, so her daughter is insisting she moves in with them.' Eliot spoke shortly, as if his mind were elsewhere. He looked at Natalie. 'I was wondering if you'd be interested in living there?'

Her heart skipped a beat, as she remembered what he'd said about making other arrangements when the baby was born.

'By myself?'

His mouth tightened. 'No, I'd planned on living there too, although the house is probably big enough for us to maintain separate establishments, if that's what you want.'

'I didn't say that.' She began to turn over the photographs. 'Poor Mrs Grosvenor! She'll miss her home, and her lovely garden.'

'Well, think about it, and let me know if you'd like to look round it at least. It hasn't come on the market yet in the strictest sense, so we have a few days' leeway. Certainly, we can't go on living here. For one thing, it won't be big enough when the baby comes. And for another...' He stopped abruptly.

'Yes?' Natalie shuffled the photographs back into the envelope, not looking at him.

Eliot was silent for a moment, then he said, 'Before we were married, I said there were no ghosts here. It was a typically arrogant remark, and I apologise for it, because it's evident that this place does have—hang-ups from the past for you that I've totally failed to exorcise.' His eyes met hers. 'You'd cleared away every physical trace of him—of your life together. You weren't even wearing his ring when I met you—but Drummond's shadow still hangs over you, doesn't it?'

Natalie sighed harshly. 'Yes,' she admitted, 'I— suppose it does.'

He nodded. 'I can't—I don't blame you for that. You were his wife. Perhaps he showed you a different side of himself from the one he displayed to the rest of the world.' He paused, his face hardening. 'Maybe if I'd been able to like him, I could understand this—continuing loyalty of yours. But he wouldn't want you to mourn for ever—to waste all your warmth and spirit on a dead man.' He took a breath. 'I swore to myself I wouldn't pressure you—that I'd give you all the time you needed.' He laughed harshly. 'I hadn't realised what sheer hell trying to be noble could be! I don't know how much longer I can take this—non-life we're living.'

The bleak words jolted Natalie like a blow to the ribs. She stared at him incredulously, her lips parting in wonder. She said slowly, 'Is—that what you think?' then stopped, as a laughing voice floated up the stairs.

'Eliot my boy, where the hell are you hiding? Come down and show me this devil horse I'm to ride for you!'

The breath was expelled explosively from Eliot's lungs. 'Calum,' he said with resignation. He got up from the table, giving Natalie a frowning, questioning look as he went to the door. 'We're up here, Cal!'

Calum Carmichael came into the kitchen like a breath of vibrant breeze. 'Well, Mrs Lang.' He grabbed Natalie's hand and raised it to his lips. 'So you're the poor soul who has the job of turning this reprobate into an honest man. God, Eliot, but your good taste is sickening!'

Natalie's head was whirling, her emotions in chaos, but a bubble of reluctant laughter escaped her. Calum's buoyant charm was irresistible.

Eliot was grinning too. 'Subtle as ever, I see! The devil horse in question is saddled and waiting for you, my son.'

Calum whistled. 'You mean you want me to get on its back now? And I was thinking I'd make his acquaintance in the parade ring.'

'Then think again,' Eliot advised caustically. He looked over Calum's elegant tweeds with a raised eyebrow. 'Though how you expect to ride looking like an ad for Harrods men's department...'

'An envious spirit is a terrible thing,' said Calum sadly. 'As it happens, I have my gear in the car. I'll tell you what it is, Mrs Lang—this sadist only wants to put me up on this horse so I'll be thrown on my face in the mud in front of my fiancée. A nice sedate drive in beautiful countryside is what I promised the woman.'

'Please won't you call me Natalie?' She smiled at him. 'And if your fiancée's with you, where is she?'

'In the car, learning her place,' Calum said instantly. 'All fillies need the same treatment—the masterful hand on the reins, the odd touch of the whip.' He winked at Natalie. 'I say this because she's safely out of earshot, the harpy. Shall I bring her up to you, then?'

The harpy turned out to be small, chestnut-haired and curvaceous, wrapped in a fun fur. She kissed Eliot with the ease of an old friend, then turned with a shy smile to Natalie, introducing herself as Cathy Horton.

When the invitation to lunch had been proffered and accepted she immediately offered to help with the preparation.

'Aren't you coming to watch me make a fool of myself on this monster?' Calum demanded reproachfully.

'We'll come up later.' She slapped him affectionately on the rear. 'Off you go, and if you do fall off, make sure the wretched animal doesn't step on anything vital. We're getting married at the end of the jumping season,' she confided to Natalie as they were left alone.

'I hope you'll be very happy.' Natalie thought they would be. They both seemed to have open, out-going personalities, although Cathy was the quieter of the two. But the way they looked at each other, the open love accepted and returned, twisted an envious knife in her soul. She said curiously, 'Don't you worry—when Calum has to ride a difficult horse?'

'All the time,' Cathy admitted calmly. 'But it's his living, what he does, so I have to accept it.' She looked at Natalie questioningly. 'You didn't have the same problem, did you? You weren't going with Eliot when he was a jockey.'

'No.' Natalie emptied a tin of tomatoes into a bowl.

'I thought I hadn't see you around,' Cathy mused. 'I knew most of Eliot's girlfriends.'

Natalie poured olive oil into a pan and began to heat it. Trying to sound casual, she asked, 'Did you know— the girl he nearly married?'

'Camilla.' Cathy paused in her onion chopping to nod vigorously. 'Yes, I knew her, and if you ask me he had a lucky escape. She didn't like any of his friends, and we weren't keen on her either. She was hand in glove with his mother, trying to make him give up horses and become something in the City like the rest of his family. Eliot—can you imagine? She was a lovely-looking girl, though,' she added fairly. 'And very sexy—always giving Eliot looks as if she wanted him to jump on her there and then. But they didn't have much going for them apart from sex. She knew he wasn't going to give up racing and live life on her terms, and that's why she threw him over. That daft business over Michelle Laidlaw was just an excuse.'

She grinned at Natalie. 'Have I covered everything?'

Natalie flushed. 'You must think I'm awful—pumping you for information like this.' She began to brown the first cubes of meat.

'It's not awful at all. It's natural you'd want to know.' Cathy brought the onions over. 'But if you're thinking Eliot married you on any kind of rebound, forget it. He got over her with indecent haste, as Calum put it.' She looked at Natalie. 'Someone said you'd been married before, but that can't be true. You're too young.'

'I was young when I got married,' Natalie explained. 'He was a jockey too. His name was Tony Drummond. You might have known him.'

Cathy shook her head. 'Before my time, probably. Did you divorce?'

Natalie shook her head. 'He was killed in an accident.' She saw something small and pinched in Cathy's face suddenly, and added hastily, 'In a car accident. Otherwise, we would have been divorced.'

Cathy looked at her meditatively for a moment, then she said, 'Well, you'll be all right with Eliot.' She paused. 'Is that it? Shall we go up to the gallops and see how they're getting on? We can take Calum's car.'

She took her welcome for granted, Natalie realised with a pang.

She said quietly, 'Yes, why not?'

Up on the moor, the air was clear and crisp. Grantham was there standing by the Land Rover, rubbing his hands vigorously together. His brows rose when he saw the girls, but he didn't offer any strictures about their presence.

'That damned Roly just up and went,' he told Natalie grumpily. 'Not a word to anyone, Wes tells me. Serves me right for breaking my own rule and taking on a casual. Well, he needn't send for his money, because he won't get it.' He nodded at Cathy. 'Midstream's tried every trick in the book to get Calum off so far, but none of them have worked. He's almost as bonny a rider as my son-in-law,' he added kindly.

The two girls exchanged amused glances, then Cathy grabbed Natalie's arm. 'Here they come now.'

The horses swept into view at an easy, controlled canter. Midstream was trying to force the pace, but

Calum was holding him in, keeping him level with Eliot on

another black, Prince Igor.

Above the subdued thunder of the hooves on the short turf there was another sound, like the crack of a whip.

A horse screamed in pain and terror, and Prince Igor's smooth onward rush was suddenly, hideously interrupted. He plunged and reared frantically, then took off at a headlong gallop, leaving Eliot lying motionless on the ground behind him.

Natalie couldn't move. She stood, her hand at her throat, as the line of horses was pulled to a startled standstill. She was aware of nothing but Eliot, lying still. How many minutes ago had Cathy told her she didn't have the same problem now that he was no longer a jockey? she wondered stupidly.

Calum had already dismounted and was bending over him. Sudden energy filled her, and she ran, stumbling, to Eliot's side.

She said to Calum, almost whispering, 'He's dead, isn't he?'

'Like hell he is,' Cal retorted witheringly. 'You're just winded, aren't you, my boy?'

'But Prince Igor kicked him—I saw it!'

'Well, what's a little kick between friends? He's had worse,' said Calum robustly. 'Now don't you start passing out on us, girl!'

Eliot groaned, and muttered something suspiciously obscene.

'That's terrible language for a dead man.' Calum could not quite disguise the relief in his tone. 'Cuddle him, Natalie. That'll bring him round quicker than anything.'

Natalie went down on her knees beside her husband's recumbent body, lifting his head gently on to her lap.

'Eliot—look at me, darling!' There was mud on his cheek and forehead, and she began to gently wipe it away.

Eliot's eyes flickered open, and he looked up at her. 'Don't look so scared, sweetheart.' He produced the words with an obvious effort. 'These things happen. Has Wes caught that bastard yet?'

'Prince Igor?' Natalie was confused. On the perimeter of her awareness there was shouting and scuffling going on, she realised.

'No.' Eliot sat up wincing, and holding his ribs. 'The swine who shot him. An air rifle, I think.'

'So that's what it was!' Calum whistled. 'Now who'd do that to a good-natured beast like old Igor? Now if he'd shot the thug I was riding...'

Eliot's voice was stronger. 'Perhaps he thought he had.' And they exchanged glances.

'Hold hard,' said Calum suddenly. 'They've got someone.'

'And I could make an educated guess who it is.' Eliot hauled himself to his feet, then pulled Natalie up beside him. His arm round her, they waited for the struggling, blaspheming figure being dragged towards them.

'Ben Watson?' Natalie found her voice. 'You?'

'Yeah, me.' He glared at Eliot. 'And what's Mr Millionaire Strang going to say when he hears his future champion's got a pellet in him?'

'He won't hear it.' Eliot's voice was steel. 'Because it didn't happen. Your sidekick should have hung round a bit longer, then he could have told you I wasn't riding Midstream today—that his jockey was going to be up instead. And what's our mutual friend Kevin Laidlaw going to say when he hears you shot at the wrong horse?' He turned to Wes. 'Take him down to the stables and

keep him there until the police come. Has someone gone
after Igor?'

'Robbie's gone, boss.' The look Wes turned on Watson
was blood-chilling. 'Maybe we should have a shot—at
rearranging your features, you little weasel. The boss
could've been killed!'

'Pity he wasn't,' sneered Ben Watson. He sent Natalie
a gloating grin. 'Did better with your pet horse, didn't
we, you bitch!'

'You let Jasmine out?' She couldn't believe it.

'Roly did. He's my cousin, and he worked for Laidlaw
before he lost two thirds of his horses, thanks to you. I
didn't realise we looked so much alike, until *she* started
in about having seen him somewhere before. Nosey little
cow!'

Eliot's face hardened. He said curtly, 'Let go of him.'

'No!' Natalie laid an imploring hand on his arm.
'Don't hit him. He's not worth it.'

'And that's more than the truth,' said Calum with
quiet disgust. 'Leave him for the lads in blue, Eliot, for
God's sweet sake. And let's get your wife home, and
give her some brandy.'

The next few hours seemed to pass in a blur for
Natalie. She was aware of the police arriving, and statements being taken, and her father saying that the vet
had easily removed a pellet from the flank of poor bewildered Prince Igor, and he'd soon be as good as new.

She obediently drank the prescribed brandy, and ate
some of the goulash which Cathy practically forced down
her throat, but nothing seemed real. She knew that Eliot
had telephone Kevin Laidlaw and told him curtly that
Ben Watson had confessed everything, and he too would
have allegations to answer.

She found she was hugging Cathy and Calum and promising they they would all get together very soon.

Then, suddenly, everyone had gone, and the bubble of unreality which had enclosed her burst. Suddenly it was just Eliot and herself, facing each other across the fireplace of the sitting room.

She moistened dry lips with the tip of her tongue. 'Do you think Kevin Laidlaw's mad?' she asked.

Eliot shrugged. 'Desperation can drive people down some strange paths,' he said.

She nodded. 'But why Jasmine?'

'Oh, that had nothing to do with Laidlaw. That was a piece of private spite on Ben Watson's part, aimed more at you than the stables, although it caused us a lot of trouble and bad publicity.'

Natalie shuddered. 'That's sick!'

'It's a sick world.' He got up, wincing slightly. 'What a hell of a day!'

His grimace of discomfort had not been lost on her. She said, 'Eliot, shouldn't you go to the hospital for a check-up—X-rays?'

He said patiently, 'I've already told you a dozen times, I haven't broken anything. I'm just a bit bruised. Do I have to strip to prove it to you?'

'Yes,' she said baldly.

Their eyes met in a tingling silence.

Eliot's brows lifted in faint amusement. 'Here—and now?'

'Not,' Natalie swallowed bravely, 'necessarily.'

He continued to watch her, a disturbing gleam in his hazel eyes. Then he said casually, 'I think I'll have a bath, to take some of the aches away.' He added gently, 'A Scotch and soda would make an ideal accompaniment.' The parting smile he sent her was hardly more than friendly, with a touch of speculation.

Natalie gave him ten minutes, then she poured some whisky into a tumbler and added a dash of soda.

She thought as she went down the passage, He doesn't think I'll do it. He thinks I'll bottle out. But this time I can't...

The bathroom door stood invitingly ajar, and she pushed it open and walked in. Eliot was lying back in the water, eyes closed, his head pillowed in a folded towel. At her entry, he looked round, his surprise evident.

'Your drink.' Oh God, why did she have to feel so hideously shy?

'Thanks.' He extended a wet hand, clearly expecting her to bring it to him. Awkwardly, Natalie trod across the carpet and handed the tumbler to him.

He raised the glass in a mocking toast. 'You're full of surprises today, darling. First I wake up with my head in your lap, and now you're bringing me drinks in the bath. What next, I wonder?'

She flushed. 'Don't—torment me, Eliot.'

'Is that what I'm doing?' he questioned drily. 'But you didn't come here to hear me ramble on. You wanted to inspect my bruises, I believe.' He drank some of the whisky, then set the glass down on the rim of the bath, before pulling himself lithely out of the water. He pointed to some discoloration on his ribs, before turning so that she could see a dark contusion on his left hip.

'Satisfied?' His gaze met hers in undisguised challenge, as he reached casually for a towel and began to dry himself.

He was waiting for her to retreat, to back off even now.

Huskily, she said, 'You know—I'm not satisfied.'

Eliot dropped the damp towel to the floor. He picked up his robe and shrugged it on, belting the sash round his waist.

'So what do you want from me, Natalie? Sex? That's simple. I'm desperate—crazy for you, as I'm sure you know.'

She shook her head. 'I—I don't think I know anything any more. If you feel like that, then why have you left me alone all these weeks? Why haven't you...?'

'Because I was frightened,' he said harshly. 'Frightened that I'd look into your eyes and see none of the things I want to see. Frightened that you'd turn away from me, reject me like you did that first time.' He flung back his head. 'I'd rather never touch you again, Natalie, than see you consumed by guilt the next morning, because you'd been unfaithful to Tony Drummond's memory.'

Her voice shook. 'But that isn't true! I—I tried to tell you so this morning before Calum arrived. Perhaps Tony does haunt me, but not in the way you think.'

He reached out and took her hand in his. 'Come and tell me about it,' he invited gently.

At the bedroom door, Natalie hesitated, but Eliot drew her past it, and down to the kitchen. He seated her at the kitchen table, then went to the refrigerator and poured her a glass of chilled milk.

'Here.' He set the glass in front of her, before seating himself opposite to her. 'Keep your strength up with this. Now tell me about Drummond.'

She sipped the milk. 'You—said you didn't like him. Will you tell me why?'

'I'd prefer not to. I'd already broken faith with myself by saying that much.' He paused. 'Why did you marry him?'

'Because he asked me,' she confessed, staring down at the table. 'I'd only recently left school. I'd never really had a proper boyfriend, and Tony—just swept me off my feet.' She laughed awkwardly. 'That's a terrible cliché.'

'It can happen.' Eliot's eyes never left her face. 'But eventually one's feet generally touch the ground again. Is that what happened?'

She nodded. 'It—it was all a sham. He didn't love me, he was just setting up a future for himself. He thought as Grantham's son-in-law he'd be the natural choice to take over at Wintersgarth eventually. And it would probably have happened. Grantham—liked him.'

'Did Drummond tell you this?'

'I managed to work it out for myself. He soon got bored with pretending to be the devoted bridegroom.' Natalie bit her lip. 'He—still fancied me, I suppose. During the first months, he—never left me alone.' She shuddered uncontrollably. 'I tried to be—the sort of wife he wanted—really I did.'

'He didn't give you pleasure?'

She said with an effort, 'He said it was my fault, that there was something lacking in me. That I was frigid. I—I bored him.'

'Was that when he started playing around?'

She looked at him, startled. 'You knew about that?'

Eliot said expressionlessly, 'He had a very big mouth. Let's leave it at that.'

'At first he was quite discreet,' she explained. 'But after a while, he couldn't be bothered. He met this woman, who was a little bit older than he was. She was divorced and had plenty of money. He bought her a lot of expensive things, and paid for them with the money in our joint account. I didn't know until the bank rang and said they couldn't put through my cheque for the electricity bill because there weren't any funds, and we'd already exceeded our agreed overdraft. I—I didn't even know we had one. When Tony came home, I tackled him, and we had a terrible row. He said if I was short of money, I should ask my father. I—told him to go. He was on his way to Jan when he was killed.'

'No wonder you reacted as you did when Grantham started pushing us together,' he remarked. 'You must have thought I was tarred with the same brush—that I looked on you as an extra asset to be acquired with my share of the stables.' He shook his head. 'God forgive me, I didn't realise your self-esteem was so low!' His voice roughened. 'Do you never look at yourself, my lady, my love? Don't you know how beautiful you are, how utterly desirable?'

She stared at the table. 'But I'm not your type.'

He said gently, 'Natalie, from the moment I saw you, I was lost. It had never happened to me before—that genuine *coup de foudre*. I couldn't believe you didn't feel it too. When you were so hostile, it was like a slap in the face. And yet when we were in the tack room, and I kissed you, I was almost overwhelmed by what I felt for you. I thought—I could take her now, and she wouldn't stop me.' He laid a hand over hers. 'That's true, isn't it?'

Natalie said wonderingly, 'Yes—oh yes!' She gave him a wavering smile. 'But I was disgusted with myself. I'd never felt anything for Tony, and I thought I loved him. You, I disliked.'

'So I gathered,' he said drily. 'I went back to Harrogate, trying to figure out whether you were an angel or just a plain hellcat. When I couldn't reach a decision,

I tried to get you out of my system in the most practical manner I could devise.'

'Your Page Three girl,' said Natalie with a little sigh.

'I could have strangled Andrew for spilling the beans about her,' he said grimly. 'I was very unfair to poor Lynn. She was quite shrewd enough to realise she didn't have my—undivided attention, and be hurt by it. And you continued to play havoc with my love life. Whenever I took another girl out, I started fantasising about you.'

He shook his head. 'And when I came up here, it all got worse. Sharing an office with you, and having you treat me like a leper, was sheer torture. Every time you pushed your hair out of your eyes, or crossed your legs, I broke out in a cold sweat. But by then I'd realised it was more than physical. I wanted all of you, heart, soul and mind. And I wanted to be everything in the world to you as well. It killed me to know that you'd belonged to Drummond first.'

She said, 'I never did—not in the way you think.'

'I know that now. And that first time in bed with you, I wondered. Because there were moments when you seemed so—surprised—so bewildered by pleasure that I might have been the only man you'd ever known.' He sighed. 'I honestly never meant to seduce you that night, Natalie. I had a plan of campaign all mapped out without one reference to bed in it. My only chance of getting you to care for me seemed to be—making you see me as a human being instead of a lust-crazed zombie.

'An old-fashioned courtship was what I had in mind. I thought, "She wants to be more involved in the training side. Well, I can arrange that, and maybe she'll be grateful to me. That would be a start." That day at the races was meant to be a cautious step in the right direction.' He grimaced. 'But I didn't bargain for finding you so—sweet and willing in my arms. It was like being handed paradise, gift-wrapped, and I couldn't resist it.' He paused. 'When you were asleep, I lay looking at you, and telling myself that you had to be in love with me— that you couldn't have given yourself like that if you hadn't cared for me. So I decided to condense the courtship into twenty-four hours, and ask you to marry me over breakfast. Only, in the event, there was no breakfast.' He groaned. 'God, I thought I'd blown it completely, lost you for ever, and I only had myself to blame. I didn't know it was possible to suffer so much. And the worst of it was I had to endure weeks of you behaving as if the most wonderful night of my life had been some bloody social misdemeanour, never to be referred to again.'

'I was in shock,' she admitted. 'I had—literally—never behaved like that in my life. Through you, I'd discovered a whole new side to my personality which until then I'd denied existed. I was too shaken to be grateful.' She was silent for a moment. 'Did it never occur to you that you might have made me pregnant?'

'It did indeed,' he said. 'But as it was practically the only accusation you didn't hurl at me that morning, I decided that you must be on the Pill, or something. I didn't really suspect until the morning you were ill. And then when I went through the post...' His mouth tightened. 'I thought, "She'll marry me now, if I have to kidnap her first." I considered waiting a few days to see if you turned to me of your own accord, but I knew in my heart that you wouldn't, so I took the initiative.'

'I hated you for that,' Natalie said in a low voice.

Eliot cupped her face tenderly in his hands. 'I didn't like myself very much. But I wanted you at any price, so I couldn't complain.

'The run-up to the wedding was murder. You obviously couldn't bear to be alone with me, which didn't augur well for the honeymoon, even if it was going to be the fairly platonic affair I'd planned. I was going to treat you very gently—just persuade you to trust me enough to share a bed with me, nothing more. I thought if you got used to sleeping with me, eventually you might want more.'

'Then—why did you turn away from me that second night?'

'Because you were scared witless,' he said bluntly. 'I touched you, and you started shaking like a leaf. I thought, "I'm supposed to love her, and I'm doing this to her!"'

Natalie said, 'I wasn't frightened of you, Eliot. Only of myself. I suppose even then I knew that I loved you, but I wouldn't admit it. I was terrified of failing again—of failing you.' She swallowed. 'If I'm honest, I'm still frightened.'

Eliot said, 'My sweet love, you can't fail. You're the other half of me, don't you know that?' He walked round the table and lifted her to her feet, smiling into her eyes. He whispered, 'Come with me, now.'

In the bedroom, he removed her clothes slowly and tenderly, pausing, as he laid each garment aside, to kiss her and caress her body. When she was naked, he held her away from him and looked at her for a long moment, his eyes so warm and loving that she felt the last traces of shyness and uncertainty dissolve away.

He said softly, 'With my body I thee worship.'

He was gentle with her at first, showing deliberate restraint, until she showed him with her hands and her mouth that she was no longer afraid—that her need, her craving for him was as intense as his for her.

She moaned with joy as her body opened for him, closed round him. Locked together, lips drinking from each other, arms and legs entwined, they rediscovered together the rhythms of love which belonged to them alone, remembered how to draw out their mutual pleasure almost to the edge of pain.

He'd called her his other half, but now both halves were melded together to become exquisitely, shatteringly one.

A thousand sensations, each one more intense than the last, were blooming, coming to flower inside her. Natalie was burning, melting, consumed in a white heat of delight. And just before existence ceased to exist altogether, she called out his name, and heard him answer her.

Slackened, totally pliant, she lay in his arms, her mouth touching the curve of his shoulder, while her index finger drew little dreamy patterns on his chest. She said, 'How did I ever think I could live without you?'

'You didn't—not seriously,' said Eliot, eyes closed. 'You just took longer to realise it than I'd hoped.' He paused. 'Of course, dear Oriel's intervention didn't help.'

'When I saw you kissing her, I wanted to die.' She added fiercely, 'I wanted her to die!'

'Actually,' he said, 'she was kissing me, and if you'd stayed a second longer, you'd have seen me step away from her.'

'But you accepted her invitation to dinner,' she protested.

'For us both,' he reminded her quietly. 'I couldn't believe it when you refused to go with me. It was as if you were pushing me into her arms.'

'But you went just the same.' Natalie's mouth twisted in remembered pain.

'Darling.' Eliot rolled over, kissing her deeply and passionately. 'Of course I had to go. She was an owner, and I reckoned she was entitled to that courtesy, but that was all. During the evening she let it be known that she wanted me to take up again where her last lover had left off, and I declined politely. She said she was sure I'd change my mind, and if I didn't she'd take her horses away. I said she must do as she pleased. It was a pretty short meal.'

'Sharon said that was why she'd done it,' said Natalie thoughtfully.

'My God!' Eliot stared at her half appalled, half amused. 'I'm beginning to be glad she left. I don't think I care to have my—sexual proclivities discussed in the yard—especially by my wife.'

She made a penitent face, running her hand slowly down his body, lingering. 'In future I'll discuss them only with you, darling.'

He gasped. 'When can the next round of talks begin?'

'As soon as you like.' She arched delicately against him, then gasped in turn. 'Heavens, as soon as that?'

This time it was a warm and leisurely coming together, like being rocked on some tideless sea in each other's arms.

'How can it be so different, and yet so wonderful?' Natalie marvelled drowsily, as the world steadied to its normal pace.

'Because I'm a genius, and not just with horses,' Eliot returned promptly, snuggling her into his arms and resting his chin on her chair.

'The conceit of you!' she laughed. 'Just be glad your ribs are bruised already!'

'I am—very glad,' he said. 'One minute I was being trodden into the ground, the next, I was lying in your arms. I began to think—maybe there's hope. Perhaps she does care for me a little.

'More than a little.' She held him tightly. 'Oh, Eliot, if I'd lost you...'

'Hush, darling.' His lips brushed her hair. 'You didn't lose me. Instead we found each other at last.'

'Yes.' She was silent for a moment. Then, 'Did you mean what you said about letting me help with the training?'

'Yes,' he said. 'But not while you're pregnant. It wouldn't be fair to Grantham.'

She turned to look up at him. 'Is there something I don't know?'

Eliot said gently, 'It was your mother, darling. She loved to be round the horses, even though your father had begged her to be careful. There was an accident one day, and she was badly kicked. That's why she lost the baby, and eventually died. It explains why Grantham's always been so over-protective with you. He's always been terrified that history might repeat itself. He kept saying to me, "She's all I've got".'

'Oh!' Her voice was distressed. 'Poor Daddy! Why did he never tell me?'

'I think he still finds it too painful—blames himself in some way for what happened. He never intended telling me—it slipped out by chance during the row we were having over his insistence on hiring a new secretary. I said it would break your heart to have to give up work so soon, and he got agitated—and out came the truth.' He kissed her lightly. 'But we'll talk him round between us. Anyway, I have a feeling he's seriously considering permanent retirement, at Beattie's request. And then, of course, I'll be the one who needs a partner. A working partner, of course,' he went on almost idly, as his hand sought her breast, tantalising its hardening peak. 'I seem to be reasonably well catered for in other—er—respects. Did you say something, my beloved?' he added solicitously, as Natalie choked.

'No.' Her voice quivered with love and amusement. 'But I expect I'll think of a few things—over the next fifty years or so.'

Eliot wrapped her even closer in his arms. 'You've been reading my plan of campaign,' he murmured contentedly, and kissed her again.

What readers say about Harlequin romance fiction...

"I absolutely adore Harlequin romances!
They are fun and relaxing to read, and
each book provides a wonderful escape."
—N.E.,* Pacific Palisades, California

"Harlequin is the best in romantic reading."
—K.G.,* Philadelphia, Pennsylvania

"Harlequins have been my passport to the
world. I have been many places without
ever leaving my doorstep."
—P.Z.,* Belvedere, Illinois

"My praise for the warmth and adventure
your books bring into my life."
—D.F.,*Hicksville, New York

"A pleasant way to relax after a busy day."
—P.W.,* Rector, Arkansas

*Names available on request.

Six exciting series for you every month... from Harlequin

Harlequin Romance·
The series that started it all

Tender, captivating and heartwarming...
love stories that sweep you off to faraway places
and delight you with the magic of love.

◆

Harlequin Presents·
Powerful contemporary love
stories...as individual as the
women who read them

The No. 1 romance series...
exciting love stories for you, the woman of today...
a rare blend of passion and dramatic realism.

◆

Harlequin Superromance®
It's more than romance...
it's Harlequin Superromance

A sophisticated, contemporary romance-fiction
series, providing you with a longer,
more involving read...a richer mix of complex plots,
realism and adventure.

Harlequin
American Romance™
Harlequin celebrates the American woman...

...by offering you romance stories written about American women, by American women for American women. This series offers you contemporary romances uniquely North American in flavor and appeal.

◆

Harlequin Temptation ™

Passionate stories for today's woman

An exciting series of sensual, mature stories of love...dilemmas, choices, resolutions... all contemporary issues dealt with in a true-to-life fashion by some of your favorite authors.

◆

Harlequin Intrigue™

Because romance can be quite an adventure

Harlequin Intrigue, an innovative series that blends the romance you expect... with the unexpected. Each story has an added element of intrigue that provides a new twist to the Harlequin tradition of romance excellence.

Harlequin Books